RED FINGER:
SECOND-HAND DEATH
AND OTHER STORIES

SECOND-HAND DEATH
AND OTHER STORIES

By Arthur Leo Zagat

POPULAR PUBLICATIONS • 2023

PUBLISHING HISTORY

"Second-Hand Death" originally appeared in the October, 1934 (Vol. 2, No. 3) issue of *Operator 5* magazine. "Death Rides the Sound" originally appeared in the November, 1934 (Vol. 2, No. 4) issue of *Operator 5* magazine. "Red Finger—Death Dealer" originally appeared in the December, 1934 (Vol. 3, No. 1) issue of *Operator 5* magazine. "Caged Horror" originally appeared in the April, 1935 (Vol. 4, No. 1) issue of *Operator 5* magazine. "Death's Red Finger" originally appeared in the September, 1935 (Vol. 5, No. 1) issue of *Operator 5* magazine. "Red Finger Meets his Match" originally appeared in the March, 1936 (Vol. 6, No. 4) issue of *Operator 5* magazine. "Red Finger—Spy Poison" originally appeared in the June, 1936 (Vol. 7, No. 2) issue of *Operator 5* magazine. "Locked in With Death" originally appeared in the August, 1936 (Vol. 7, No. 3) issue of *Operator 5* magazine. "Death's Toy Shop" originally appeared in the January, 1937 (Vol. 8, No. 2) issue of *Operator 5* magazine. "Envoy of Doom" originally appeared in the July, 1937 (Vol. 9, No. 2) issue of *Operator 5* magazine. "The Spy Who Stole Death" originally appeared in the September, 1937 (Vol. 9, No. 3) issue of *Operator 5* magazine. "Red Finger's Murder Messenger" originally appeared in the March, 1938 (Vol. 10, No. 2) issue of *Operator 5* magazine. "Red Finger and the Murder Trio" originally appeared in *The Spider: Slaughter, Incorporated (Facsimile Edition)* (2018). Copyright 2018 by Argosy Communications, Inc. All rights reserved.

SECOND-HAND DEATH

THERE IS nothing to distinguish Duane's Second-hand Bookstore from the other shops of its kind that line lower Fourth Avenue with their decrepit outside-boxes of tattered volumes in front of their dark bookstacks within. Its signs— "This Box 15¢ Each"; "Choice Selections, 50¢"—are just as rain-streaked and illegible, its grimed plate-glass just as forlorn. As pathetic, too, the men and women with worn faces and thread-bare garments who dare its gloomy precincts to browse along those musty shelves.

Nor is there anything to set him apart from the other store-keepers the long-faced, alpaca-coated man who inhabits its depths—as dusty-seeming and inconspicious as his stock-in-a-very-paltry-trade, except that he appears a bit younger than the others, and that his very blue eyes are continually moving and very watchful.

And yet, death and the fear of death are a living presence in that drab shop.

The shadows that lie in black pools on the unpainted floor might well be the brooding shadows of world-events stirring heavily in the womb of time; the dirt-streaked curtains at the rear that part occasionally to show a narrow camp-cot, a wooden chair, and a two-burner gas-plate on an upended box, might be the veil that hides a nation's fate. For Ford Duane is not quite

1

what he seems, though his very existence depends on the main-tenance of his identity as a dreamy, cobweb-brained sexton of a Tomb of Defunct Books.

Surely the bent old man, in a frock coat of rusty black, and high, clean stock over which his grayish chin folds and quivers, who hugs a dog-eared volume in his gaunt fingers, cannot have picked this particular doorway in which to stand timorously for any other cause but chance. He had tottered slowly down the long block, pausing momentarily at each cluttered entrance, palpably working up courage to pass through one of them. His bleared old eyes blink and peer nearsightedly at Duane as he silently appears from the shadows almost as though one of them had come to life.

The ancient gulps. "I—I—You buy old books, do you not?" he quavers.

A secret smile flickers around the other's suprisingly firm, determined mouth. "Occasionally," he responds, "Though I prefer to sell them. What have you there?"

"A Petronius, printed by Arden and bound by Trant." He says it proudly, and hearer's dark eyebrows arch as if in appreciation, but, curiously enough, there was never any such printer as Arden nor any binder as Trant. Is Ford Duane a neophyte then, to be impressed by unctuously mouthed but counterfeit names? Is the would-be seller a fraud? Perhaps. And then again....

"Let me see it." Duane takes the book from the reluctant hand of the old man, riffles its yellow pages. The leather of its binding smears his fingers with a fine brown dust. "Yes," he says at last. "It is a fine specimen, but I can only offer you two dollars for it."

"Two dollars! It cost me twenty-five!" And so starts a leisurely chaffering on the doorstep, where any passerby can hear. And why not? They have nothing to hide, those two....

Nothing?

The bargaining is over at last, the book is Duane's. As he counts the money into a palsied palm, he watches the old man falter down the street, vanishing around the nearest corner. Then he turns back into his shop.

Those extraordinarily keen eyes of his flick over the two or three idlers as he moves slowly toward the rear. His thin, aquiline face is impassive, but an exceedingly close observer might notice that a tiny muscle is twitching in his smooth cheek. He goes through the curtain that ineffectually conceals his living quarters from the store proper and it drops behind him. Momentarily, at least, he is concealed from those outside. He rests a hand on a breast-high book-filled shelf; there is a flicker of movement—and he has vanished!

BEHIND THOSE shelves that have swung out and back on oiled hinges so quickly, Ford Duane is no longer impassive. By the light of a small bulb high up in the ceiling his face is alive and his eyes glow with excitement.

The book he has just purchased is still in his hand, he lays it on a shelf that is attached to the inner wall, opens it to the first blank flyleaf. Seating himself on a high stool, he pulls out a drawer beneath the shelf, fumbles out of it a tiny hooded lamp that he sets next to the leather covered Petronius. He plugs the short cord attached into a socket before him, reaches to a handy switch.

Click! The ceiling bulb goes out and velvety, impenetrable darkness invades the cubicle. *Click!* That was the sound of another switch, but the blackness remains, so thick as to be almost tangible. There must be something wrong with the wiring of the little lamp.

No! There, just where the book must be, tiny wriggles of light appear, iridescent tracery of living fire. Indistinct at first their outlines become clearer. They are letters, words. Exhaled breath hisses sharply as Ford Duane reads the message that has come to him thus deviously from an inner, closely-barred and guarded room in a certain building in faraway Washington.

A solution of aspirin, a ball-pointed pen, were all that were required to write that invisible communication. A special bulb, equipped to emit only ultra-violet light was all that was needed to make it give up its secret.

But a man will die tonight, before Duane can act on the instructions thus given him. A man will die and horrible death will hover over hundreds, thousands more. Tomorrow a coded cable will flash under two oceans and bring consternation into another barred and guarded room in a chancellery three thousand miles from the one in Washington....

A BLACK shade was tightly drawn over the window of a small room on the twentieth floor of the St. Vincent Hotel. The towering façade outside this aperture dropped sheer and ledgeless from its sill. Only a fly could have found hand- or foot-hold, on that blank wall, and so far did the huge hostelry overtop the surrounding low roofs that the interior of the chamber could be observed only from the spidery structure of Brooklyn Bridge, a quarter-mile away, and then only by a powerful spy-glass.

But the room's occupants seemed to have great need of secrecy, for its door was locked, not only by its usual bolt but also by a contrivance that slid between door-edge and jamb and could be removed without trace. The crevices around the door and its keyhole were tightly stuffed with cotton batting, and the single light within was cast by a lamp whose shade was covered with a black cloth. Its illumination was thrown only downward to the table-top on which it stood.

The rest of the room, therefore, was in semi-darkness enhanced somehow by the pale gleam of the bed's coverlet and the darker shadows of two men seated opposite one another at the table.

Only their hands were clearly visible.

One pair clutched the edge of the small round table. They were big hands, their joints swollen, the tips and inner surfaces of their fingers calloused as only long, hard labor can harden a man's skin. They were weather-tanned, but under the bronze there was a gray pallor oddly at variance with their evident strength. The palms were wet with cold sweat.

The owner of these hands, one knew, was under a tremendous strain, was fighting hard to keep an appearance of steadiness and calm while he waited for some critical decision to be made by the other.

The hands of that other, slim and effeminate, conveyed an impression of wily power, of sure dominance. Their skin was oddly tinged, the nails filed to queer long points, and at the base of those nails, crescents of deep blue, strangely exotic.

These hands gripped the margins of the topmost blueprint of a pile spread over the top of the table. One felt, rather than saw, that the owner of those hands was intently absorbing every quirk and angle of the sharply defined white lines that patterned the cerulean sheet.

Within the circle of illumination there were two other objects, both close to the hands holding the outspread plan. One was a bulky package of grimy-edged, rumpled envelopes held by a thick, black elastic. The other was a bull-nosed automatic, compact and vicious.

For a while there was no sound in that mysteriously isolated chamber except the faint rustle of paper and the heavy, tortured breathing of the man who waited. Then his vis-à-vis spoke. "Yes," he muttered, "These are what I wanted, Mister Lassiter. You have fulfilled your bargain."

"How about your end, then?" Lassiter asked hoarsely. "The letters—?"

"Are yours," The speaker's hand moved swiftly, yet without hurry, to the automatic's grip. It lifted the gun and pushed the bundle of letters across the table with its muzzle. They vanished in Lassiter's capacious paw, now visibly trembling, "You may assure the lady her secret is safe."

"Damn it, Odon," There was a wealth of bitterness in the response, "that's the only way you'd have ever gotten those plans of the subway ventilating system from me. If they'd been my own letters I'd have told you where to go, but I couldn't let hers get to—"

"The person who would have been so very interested in reading them. No! We knew that, and used our information." Odon was rolling the plans up dextrously, though one yellow hand still held the automatic. "I cannot quite comprehend your Occidental viewpoint."

"You wouldn't. But I still can't get it through my head why you went to so much trouble to get them. The principles are common knowledge, and your engineers—"

"ARE AS good as yours. Yes." Something vaguely mocking

7

had come into Sato's tone. "Perhaps you might be enlightened if I were to tell you that I represent not the municipality of our largest city but—our War Office."

"What!" Lassiter forgot caution in an astonished shout. "Your War—But why—?"

"Why should that department be interested in your subway?" A chair grated as the alien rose. "Simply this, my dear sir. While our King and your President struggle to reach an approachment on the difficulties between our nations, we of the military prepare for the failure of their negotiations. New weapons are being forged on both sides, new methods of warfare. No longer will the uniformed forces alone bear the brunt of battle. The new strategy will consist of striking at the civilian population, and striking first. Gas and disease germs, will be munitions of the next war, their swift dissemination will constitute its tactics. With these maps we shall know just where to place our gas bombs, just where to release our death-dealing microbes so that they may spread through New York with the greatest rapidity. You see—"

"*You dog!*" Lassiter's chair crashed to the floor as he leaped to his feet, the table skidded sideways as he dove past it, his big hands fisted and flailing. "*You yellow dog!*" But the other's ready gun cracked, its sound thundering here but inaudible outside the muffled room.

A sudden blue hole appeared in the engineer's right temple. Odon slid aside, catlike, watched Lassiter plunge past him and thud blindly against the wall. The big man clawed at the plaster; a sound burbled from his throat, something between a groan and a shriek. Then life was out of him and he had collapsed, a shapeless, sprawling heap on the dull maroon carpeting. Where the back of his head lay, a darker pool spread, seeped into the thick pile.

Odon stood motionless for a moment, the faintest of smiles twisting his thin lips with cold cruelty. "So to the rest of his nation when the day comes," he muttered in his own language. "And may it dawn soon."

He turned back to the table, put his murder-weapon down, and lifted the blueprint roll to stow it in a cunningly-contrived pocket of his dark jacket. "But I must rid myself of the weakness that urged me to taunt him with the fate awaiting his country-men before I stilled his tongue forever."

His long fingers sought the light chain, jerked it. Blackness swept in to hide murderer and victim under a common pall, but there was a feel of movement in the room, the slither of the spy's feet across the rug, the soft rub of cotton against wood as he pulled the muffling from the door cracks. The metal grated with the wee sound of well-oiled hinges. A widening gray line showed that the door was opening to let the spy out into the early-morning corridor with his burden of horrible death for New York's teeming millions. His squat form was silhouetted against that dimness, and then—*against a sudden blaze of white light from a flashlight lens.* "Not so fast, Odon," a cold, hard voice sounded. "Not so fast."

Low-toned as it was, that voice was keen-edged with threat of sudden death. The spy saw a gleam of metal next the steadily held flashlight, the snouting barrel of a revolver. His face froze, was an expressionless mask. His one hand tightened its hold on the doorknob till white showed over the muscle at the base of its thumb, and the other arm moved rigidly away from his side. "Get back," the newcomer ordered. "Get back into that room."

Odon's three rearward strides were stiff-legged, the newcomer's advance noiseless as the foreigner's own movements had been. The door thudded shut once more on taut drama within the drab hotel room.

The torch-beam, reflected back from palely-enameled walls showed a vague, black-clothed figure ominously motionless. A gray felt was pulled low over his forehead, a gray mask hid nose and mouth, only his narrowed eyes were revealed, their irises a steely blue. Even the one visible hand that held the butt of his weapon was covered by a skin-tight glove. That glove pulled the killer's glance to it. Concealed fear flickered in the oddly-round eyes that betrayed his race. For, although the rest of the glove was black, the finger curled around the gun's trigger was a glaring scarlet, as if it had been dipped in fresh blood.

The spy's lips scarcely moved, but his words were sharp; "The Red Finger!" was what he said. "But I thought—"

"That Reinhardt Gans had done for me? So he reported to *his* government, and your undercover man there read that report and sent the news on to you. Whereupon all you spies and *saboteurs* breathed a huge sigh of relief. It would be lots safer now, you thought, to carry on your filthy work in the United States, each for his own nation, getting ready for the time you all dream of when America will have to fight the World. But Gans was mistaken. Too bad, isn't it?"

SECOND-HAND DEATH

ODON SHRUGGED, fatalistically. "Very much too bad. We will have to take steps to repair Gans' mistake."

"I don't doubt that you will try. But in the meantime, the plans, please, for which you killed Lassiter. Put them on that table." The voice of the Red Finger was suddenly diamond-hard. "And only the plans. You know well enough that if your hand comes out with a gun in it my lead will be in your belly before you have a chance to use it."

The spy's thin lips tightened, a straight gash across his face. "Take them," he defied, "if you can."

"I'll take them from your dead body, you rat," Red Finger snapped. "In ten seconds. *One—*"

"No you won't. Look." Odon's stiffly-extended left arm twisted, so that the palm of its hand was turned toward the other. Held loosely between thumb-ball and palm a half-inch crystal ball glittered. "If my hand relaxes this will drop. It contains quintol, our new explosive, sufficient to blow everything in this room to atomic fragments. How about it, Red Finger, will you shoot?"

The American paused almost imperceptively. "*Two—,*" his count went on, "*Three—*"

Odon's queer eyes glowed. "That isn't all," he resumed, smoothly. "On my body is a thin-walled vial in which is a virulent culture of the bacilli of the bubonic plague. Shattered by the explosion, they will scatter—hundred, thousands in this city will die horribly—"

Red Finger had continued steadily through this pronouncement. "*Six—Seven—*"

What manner of man was this? The villain was not bluffing,

11

that much was certain. Nor could he be bluffed; fanatic eagerness to die for a cause is a notorious trait of his race. Was the Red Finger about to sacrifice deliberately hundreds of lives for momentary triumph, a triumph he himself could not live to savor? *"Eight—"*

The contemplated use of the plans he determined would be hardly more damaging than the result of his shot. *"Nine—"* The American's face was hidden, but Odon's glistening features, flat-faced, high cheek-boned, was set, fish-scaly beneath its racial tinge. Eternity quavered in the tiny chamber before the final numeral crackled on the taut air—*"Ten!"*

The scarlet finger jerked, a dull plod sounded, a fine mist sprayed from the American's gun muzzle, a vaporous cloud about the spy's head. His body twitched, then, was limp. His hand opened. The ball was dropping—seemed to hang in space as if reluctant to loose the cataclysm it enclosed. Lightning quick, Red Finger sprang forward, his hand darted out, was under the death-sphere! The fragile crystal nestled into a soft, gloved palm; fingers, one carmine, closed gingerly about it. Before Odon's flaccid form had thudded to the floor and settled to its final lax sprawl, the tiny murder-bomb had vanished into some interstice of the other's clothing and his revolver was back again in the queerly-marked hand that had so dexterously averted disaster. Pent breath whistled from behind the mask, and a muffled voice exclaimed, "Close, by George! Too damn' close for comfort."

Red Finger allowed himself only that instant's consideration of what would have followed failure. Then he dropped, lithely as all his motions were, to his knees beside the still form of his victim. A moment's fumbling and the long roll of blueprints was transferred to his own person. The squat automatic was next. Red Finger's hands trembled as they extracted a thin glass sliver containing a murky yellow jelly. The clipped letters that had been Lassiter's doom appeared in the fanlike beam of the counter-spy's torch. Red Finger held these for a moment, scrutinizing the handwriting. "Marie Prall," he muttered. "Back at her old tricks. If Lassiter had only known what I do about her...."

Here lay the real tragedy of this incident in the underground warfare that wages continually between spy and counter-spy in every city of the world. The woman for whom the engineer had, with woefully mistaken chivalry, sacrificed his honor and his life was an international adventuress, her services at the command of the highest bidder....

THE PACKET stowed in the capacious recesses of his garments, Red Finger turned to contemplate Odon. "I'd like to leave you here," he addressed the still figure grimly, "for the city cops to find. But your compatriot fireaters would welcome the indictment of the Baron Odon for murder in America, it might be just the spark they need to destroy the peace of the world. War's coming sooner or later, but my jobs to stave it off as long as I can." He shrugged, "And so, my dear Odon...."

Red Finger lifted himself erect, out of the glow of the torch that he had laid on the floor. Fabric rustled. A click, and the lamp came on, the black covering whisked from its shade. A red-haired youth was visible, freckled-faced and grinning, attired in the emerald green uniform of the St. Vincent's bellhops. He was twenty-two or thereabouts, his deceptively slender body concealing muscles of steel, sinews of whipcord.

He bent again, lifted the squat spy effortlessly, propelled the unconscious man toward the door. So cleverly was it done that anyone watching would have sworn that he was a hotel guest who had drunk not wisely, but too well, who was being guided to his room by an urchin half-amused, half-bored. And it was thus that the two progressed through the dim-lit hotel corridor, up a flight of stairs, and into another room directly above that in which sudden death had come to one more dupe of the new international espionage.

Here Odon was tossed, still fully dressed, on a bed. The putative bellhop did a curious thing then. He got down on the floor, squirmed under that very bed. In seconds he was out again, dragging after him a small black box from which two filament-like wires trailed. On top of the flat contrivance a perforated disk showed, the earpiece of the device that combined stethoscope and radio-amplifier to make eavesdropping a facile thing. It was evident now how he had been able to time his appearance at the psychological moment.

The youth crossed to a window, pulled it up, and hurled the contrivance out. The crash of its landing came faintly up to him, at the end of a twenty-one story fall to hard concrete. There wouldn't be enough left of the instrument to tell even a paleontologist what it had been. A last quick glance around to see if there were any other trace of his long vigil here, then the door opened and Odon was alone, sleeping stertorously on the bed where he had been placed. Peculiarly enough, when he woke in the morning he would find that the room had been registered in his name, the night's rental paid. And, very wisely, he would slink away into the vagueness of the furtive land in which he moved, nursing a headache and the sourness of defeat....

THE STOOP-SHOULDERED man with a florid face bleared by bad liquor who shambled unsteadily up a slimy tenement stoop on Third Avenue resembled neither the dusty Ford Duane who kept a bookshop on Fourth, just behind, nor the red-haired, grinning bellhop of the Hotel St. Vincent. He had trouble in finding his key, this derelict, and a watchful cop had already started to walk over from across the cartracks before the unpainted door in the dark vestibule opened. Once in the dimly-lit hallway reeking with stale smell of yesterday's corned beef and cabbage and the boiled fish of the week before, the man padded down creaking wooden steps silently, turned left between white-washed cellar walls to the shabby room that he rented from a hard-pressed janitor for a dollar a week. His hand closed on the knob of the skewed door. A voice said, "Hold it that way, you. Just that way."

The man froze. From the shadows beyond, two forms materialized. Rough fingers clutched his arms, digging in. "Chees, guys," the bum whined, "yer shinnying the wrong pole. I ain't got a jit, honest I ain't."

A guttural chuckle sounded, then a second voice said, thickly, "You might so well not try that, Chohn O'Hara. Or maybe you like better that I call you Red Finger? Save your breath for a prayer, because your tricks are all through."

The Bowery accent dropped from the captive's speech, and

he slumped wearily, the hands holding him apparently his only support. "Oscar Thorn!" he groaned in defeat, "you—" His speech choked suddenly, and he exploded into action. One foot lifted behind, lashed out and plunked into a soft groin. And Duane's left arm was free.

His hand flashed to a armpit; a knife gleamed in the dimness. He whirled, and steely muscles ripped away from the other retaining clutch. His quick twist showed him a second blade sweeping down at him. He caught it on his own, parried it with consummate skill. His opponent, bulky, obese, grunted, dodged back, came in again with surprising agility. But the American's muscles vibrated like tempered springs, he flashed in and out again—and the battle was over. A heavy form thudded to broken concrete.

Ford Duane whipped to the other man squirming on the basement floor. A pencil ray shot from a thin torch in his hand, kicked a brutish face out of the darkness, blue-jowled. He studied that face for a fleeting instant, came to a quick decision. "You," he snapped. "Do you know what this is all about?"

The fellow groaned. "Cripes," he blurted. "No! De guy asks me does I want ter make a sawbuck beatin' a guy up an' I says I'd work over me own gran'mudder fer dat. Den he brings me in here an' we lays fer yuh. Gawd, if I'd knowed...."

"All right," Duane interrupted. "That's all I want to know. You can make that ten yet, and another like it if you will do as I say, and keep your mouth shut."

"Gawd," the other grunted, unbelievingly. "Ye're an all right guy at that. What've I get ter do?"

A HALF-HOUR later there was a new-made grave in the soft dirt of the tenement's backyard. A bewildered gorilla was climbing a fence on the way to freedom. Duane watched his shadowy form disappear in the graying dawn, sighed, and turned wearily back into the basement.

Once more he was at the door of the cellar room that had once been a coal-bin. That door thudded softly behind him, and his tired footsteps seemed recurring echoes of that thud in the windowless dark. A bedstead creaked, hinges grated softly. And there was no longer anyone in that other room.

But—moments later—Ford Duane was in the concealed cubicle behind his bookshop. Deft fingers twitched off a wig, erased skillfully applied paint, removed collodion strips that had widened nostrils, broadened a thin mouth. A flicker of movement, and a pajamaed young man moved slowly about his meagre living quarters, donning the dusty habiliments of a dreaming, other-wordly bookseller.

No one would wonder if he dozed off at his pamphlet-cluttered desk out there between the bookshelves. He always looked as if he were half-asleep anyway.

DEATH RIDES THE SOUND

THE SHABBY stores along lower Fourth Avenue are somehow furtive despite the apparent frankness of their decrepit outside-boxes of "Bargains in Used Books." A film of gritty dust grimes these bedraggled offerings, smuts the unwashed window-fronts, seeps into the gloomy interiors of the shops and spreads gray haze over the absorbed browsers and somnolent attendants within. Those who frequent the vicinity know, or think they know, that its air of hangdog stealth cloaks neither sly criminality nor high intrigue, that it is rather the pitiable camouflage of outlived writings, and of men who have never known life.

Nowhere, perhaps, is there a drowsier back-eddy of musty quiet and stagnant uneventfulness than this. Yet, over one of the drab shops in this sleepy row the scythe of Death is suspended by a spider-filament taut to the breaking point. The merest whisper of suspicion into the ear of one of a half-score thin-lipped, stony-faced men sitting behind the guarded doors of secret rooms in far-off capitals would map that thread. The slightest hint reaching one of a hundred others; ghostly wraiths waging unacknowledged war in the dim underways of a world ostensibly at peace; and eager fingers would reach thousands of miles to sever its tenuous fibre. For something more than the life of a man hangs by that easily parted strand. A Nation's fate depends on its strength.

Death, and the fear of death are silent, invisible sentinels at either side of the pamphlet-hung doorway in which Ford Duane folded his lanky limbs into a broken-backed swivel chair. Beneath their drooping lids his very blue eyes freeze suddenly to icy points and the scalp tightens under his brown shock of unruly hair. The glance of a passerby has lingered a fraction of a second too long on his spare frame!

Lithe muscles coil like steel springs, thin nostrils flare imperceptibly... but the paunchy man with the rusted-black derby shambles on and Duane relaxes. He knows there is nothing to fear from this particular individual; but how he *knows*, he cannot tell you. There is a sixth sense common to a hunter and hunted by which they recognize each other's presence. And as both hunter and hunted, Ford Duane possesses that sense to a marked degree....

His head turns slowly to a tinny rattle from up the avenue. Its source is revealed as a leisurely approaching pushcart, piled high with gleaming kitchen utensils and shoved by a stocky, shirt-sleeved and sweating man. As Duane spies the portable store a raucous voice calls out: "Pails, axes, teenvare. Pails, axes, teenvare." The corner of the bookseller's mouth quirks.

A bent old woman, Victorian bonnet fastened to the straggly gray remnants of her hair by that almost obsolete instrument, a hat-pin, appears from the interior of his shop. One almost transparent claw grips a dog-eared volume of Jane Porter's *Thaddeus of Warsaw* and a professional gleam comes into Duane's eye as he slouches erect, scenting a sale. "I can let you have that for…" he begins, but his face falls as the supposed customer squeaks, "Oh, I just want to get a pail from the man; my old one sprang a leak this morning."

"By Jove," the bookseller exclaims, "so did mine! Maybe we can get them cheaper if one of us buys two at a time. Here, you wait and let me get them."

"Pails, axes, teenvare," the peddler's shout is repeated. He has other items in his cart, but his cry is unvarying. Does it convey any meaning to Duane? Is it merely coincidence that the same initial letters recur now in the pushcart man's shout? "*P*ails, *a*xes, *t*eenvare." Perhaps. But the shopkeeper's stroll to the curb is too nonchalant, too open to have an ulterior meaning. Duane scarcely glances at the pails the peddler hands him at last, certainly they are twins, and the one he turns over to the old woman in exchange for her twenty-two cents is taken at random. DUANE MOVES through his shop with no apparent haste. He pauses to straighten a shelf and the shining bucket whose bail he has thrust over his arm clangs against its edge. But, veiled by the lax droop of their lids, Duane's eyes slide over the idlers in the shadows, discreet challenge in their hazed depths. Only the old, familiar figures lurk in the shadows. A tiny muscle twitches in Duane's smooth cheek and he reaches the half-open curtain swinging before the narrow alcove. There, only a rumpled camp cot and a two-burner gas plate indicate his living quarters. He turns to the right, is momentarily hidden from the store-room beyond. A slender wall of tight-packed books moves suddenly on well oiled hinges, swings back into place.

The incident is lightning-fast. The musty alcove is just as it was before. Except that Ford Duane has vanished from it.

Behind that wall of shelved books is a cramped, windowless cubicle, not more than a yard square. When Duane seats himself on a high stool and sets the pail, top down, on a narrow wooden ledge attached to the inner wall, a fair-sized rat would have trouble finding room to squeeze in. A switch clicks and a powerful light, high up in the ceiling, pours down its radiance. The man's sharp-edged face is no longer impassive. His eyes are ablaze with excitement and eagerness, his thin lips half parted. His long-fingered hand trembles slightly as he pulls out a drawer beneath the shelf and extracts from it a jeweler's magnifying glass.

Fitting the lens into his right eye, Duane bends over

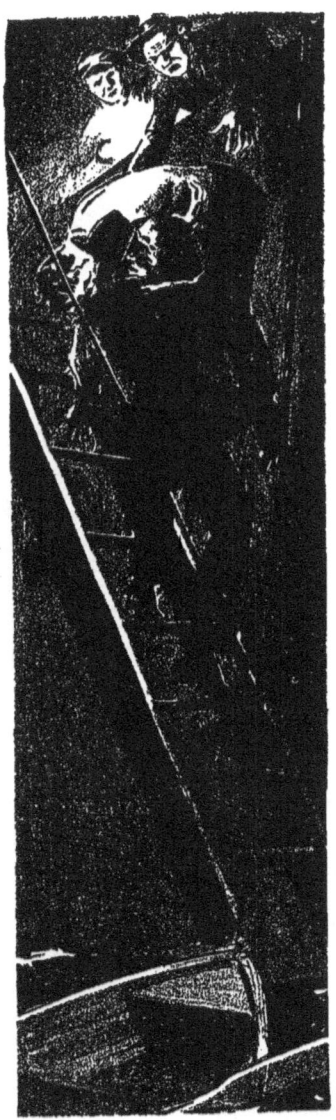

21

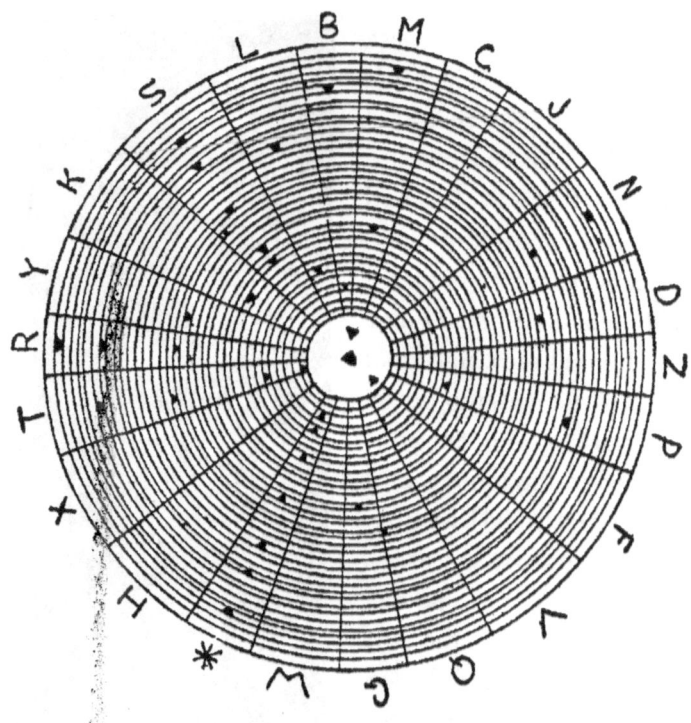

the tin bucket, and scrutinizes its upturned bottom. Faint breath hisses from between his teeth and his hands tighten on the shelf edge. But the powerful light beating down on the tin disk reveals only a number of almost microscopic indentations, scattered at random over its shiny surface, tiny, pointed scratches such as no polished surface can escape, no matter how carefully it be handled.

The pseudo-bookman reaches for the drawer again, brings out a pencil, a sheet of paper, and another object. It is a disk of transparent celluloid, and as Duane places it on the pail bottom he sees that it is engraved with a series of close, concentric circles and radiating lines. Around the outermost circumference a series of letters are etched, and a circular space at the center is blank, except for three scratches very like those on the pail, triangularly arranged. Strangely enough a little juggling of the celluloid makes the three tiny markings in the center of tin coincide with the trio on the transparent disk. Duane grunts with satisfaction.

Each of the other scratches, seen through the engraved film, falls exactly within one of the tiny arcs marked off by the whitish circles and straight lines, and no two are between the same two circles. Duane catches up his pencil and jots down letters, swiftly.

In seconds, he is staring at this cabalistic line:

SBTRS * PLN * DSTRY * GSMSK * PLT * B * T

and his face is suddenly bleak, his mouth a straight, thin gash. His pencil moves again, swiftly, putting in omitted vowels;

SABOTEURS PLAN DESTROY GASMASK PLANT B—T

Duane's lids narrow to hairline slits, and two white spots appear either side his pinched nostrils. Why has the mysterious individual known only as "T," head of the American Counter-espionage Service, sent it to him?

For a long time there is no movement in the hidden chamber, no slightest sound except the deep, even breathing of a man sunk in deep thought. On the ancient continent that lies over the blue curve of the earth and sea armies are on the march, their grim weapons charged and ready, while the dictators who have set them moving mouth-phrases about "usual maneuvers" that they do not expect to be believed. The ranks are forming, but in each bristling front there is a vacant space. Holocaust waits for America, and America, remembering what Europe would have her forget, smiles with veiled eyes and says quietly, "Not again. Once was enough!"

On a still more ancient continent another race waits with inscrutable patience for the Day when the lowering Western sun shall be bathed with the hue of blood. But some among them are not content to wait....

IN MOONLESS, misty darkness two figures paced the lightless margin of Long Island Sound. High above them the vault of a great bridge sprang in a soaring arch, behind them gigantic cylindrical tanks loomed ominously. Squat buildings leered at them from red-glowing windows, seeming somehow diabolical in the murk. But those were only the huge containers for illuminating gas that supply New York, the fires that encarnadined those windows only distilled that gas in long iron retorts of heated coal. Why then are blue-barreled rifles slanting across the shoulders of these slow-moving sentries; why should the men peer so tensely into the low-lying river haze? Why are soldiers on sentry go with loaded guns in a land at peace with all the world?

"Gees, Sarge," one of the guards voiced this very question. "I'm gettin' the gimmicks watchin' for somethin'—I don't know what. What's the big idea, haulin' the battalion off Governor's Island an' shippin' us over here? Labor trouble?"

"No. No-o-o." The free hand of the other rasped the graying bristles on his square jaw. "I dunno as I ought to tell you, but if you can keep your lips buttoned mebbe I will. You should ought to know what you're looking for. Know what you're guardin', Jenkins?"

"I'm askin' you."

The sergeant's voice was a hoarse whisper. "Gas-masks—six million gas-masks!"

"Yeah! What would we do with six million gas-masks? Hell, that's enough for every man, woman an' child in Noo Yawk."

"That's just who they're for."

The private chuckled. "Good stuff! But I ain't a rookie. C'm on, what's th' straight dope?"

"I jest give it to yuh."

"But what th' hell would we want to be puttin' masks on civvies for? Women an' kids ain't goin' to do no fightin'!...."

"But they're goin' to git gassed in the next war. Judas Priest, wake up! Don't yuh read the papers?"

"Aw, those tabloids is all guff!"

"You'd know if you'd been on guard at staff meetings, like me. I'm tellin' yuh the next war is goin' to see whole cities wiped out by gas before we get a chance to shoot off a rifle. But Uncle Sam ain't asleep. We've got gas-mask plants an' warehouses all along both seaboards, an' at the first sign of trouble the masks gets put out to everybody, damn quick. This Plant B's the biggest. Maybe they got a tip-off that it's goin' to be blown up or some-thin' tonight. That's why we're here. Orders is take any suspicious characters alive so that we can find out what country's trying the stunt."

Jenkins was convinced. "Hell," he spat. "Any country pulls

anything like that, we're going to hop all over 'em. We ain't goin' to take any more Black Toms layin' down!"

"Put my name on that detail too. I—*Hell! What's that?*"

The sergeant whirled, his rifle barrel slapping into his left palm, its butt jerking to his shoulder. *"Who is there?"* he challenged, the sharpness of his voice flatting at the river-mist.

The private was taut, his gun also at the ready. "Whatja hear?" he muttered from the corner of his mouth.

"Sounded like an oar. But I don't see nothin'. Guess mebbe it was a water rat…."

"Or some sailor heaving garbage overboard from that Eyetalian tramp over there by Ward's Island. Wonder to me they let her stay there."

"We can't tip our hand by shyin' every boat away from here. That would be a dead giveaway. Now, as I was sayin'…. *G-gaw…* ."

The sergeant choked suddenly; the rifle dropped; his hands came up to claw at his throat, were reddened by a gush of blood from a gaping hole where an instant before his neck had been. He slumped to the gravel, the private's lifeless form thudded atop him. And gray mist rolled over two twisted, gory corpses; a hazy mist-shroud that hid them with a softness more merciful than that of the men who had done this thing.

For an instant the night held its breath in shocked silence, then stone grated against wood. The shadowy keel of a rowboat dug into the gravelly beach. It rocked a bit, and two stocky figures came over the gunwale, waded ashore. One slithered to the entangled bodies, bent swiftly to them, rose as swiftly. "Both dead. That was fine shooting, Dominic."

"And the silencer worked beautifully; the alarm has not been given." The other hesitated a moment, then went on. "But I do not like it, Angelo. I tell you I do not like it. There is no war between our country and theirs. I am befouled with the murder of two brave soldiers."

"Dominic!" Angelo's voice was sharp. "You forget yourself. It is not for us to question orders, for us only to obey. Our leader, the all-wise, has set this task for us. But hurry! We have ten minutes to get our bombs from the boat, plant them and return to the *Santa Maria.*"

Dominic still temporised. "There were two sentries, not one as we were told. Perhaps there has been a leak, and the plant itself is also more thoroughly guarded."

"Bah! If I had known that you were such a coward I should have come alone. One of these is a sergeant, he but chanced to be here at the crucial moment. Come."

The two saboteurs returned to grope in the dark bulk of their boat. They straightened, each lifting a shadowy bag. And froze as cold, hard words vibrated behind them.

"Stay just that way, you two." That sudden voice was keen-edged with the threat of sudden death. "Put those bags down in the boat, gently, and your guns beside them."

The prowlers dipped to obey, lifted again. "Now turn, slowly." Oddly the speaker seemed as anxious to avoid being heard as they themselves had been, to judge from the repression of his tone, pitched so as to reach them and be heard no further. They came around stiffly till they faced their captor.

HE SEEMED at first a part of the swirling fog, so blurred were his outlines. A shapeless gray felt was pulled low over his forehead, a gray mask covered his face so that only the glint of narrowed eyes were visible through its slits. His figure was formless in a black cloak that fell from his shoulders to the ground. But that which tightened the spies' scalps and bristled the short hairs at the base of their skulls with superstitious fear was the steady hand that held a revolver point-blank at their heads.

It was black, that hand, black-gloved except for the long finger that curled around the weapon's trigger. That was scarlet; even in the misty dark they could see that glaring scarlet as if it had been dipped in fresh blood. And a name dripped like blood from Angelo's bloodless lips. "Red Finger!"

The mask head nodded, and it seemed almost as if the hidden mouth smiled humorlessly. "Red Finger," it assented, savoring the dread that name inspired among all who moved in the murky underworld of international intrigue.

A second's silence intervened, accentuated by the greasy lap of water along the rowboat's keel and the far-off melancholy hoot of a ferry. Then, "Who gave you the orders for—this?"

"Capit—" Dominic began, his voice thinned by fear, but Angelo's hard-driven elbow into his side choked off the words. "Try and find out!" the more virulent of the two said. "We have failed, and death is our reward, but we shall never talk. You will save time by turning us over to your police."

Red Finger's black shoulders shrugged. "That, precisely, is

what I shall not do. But you are small fry; I have no more time to waste on you." The scarlet digit twitched, twice. No report shattered the river quiet, but two jets of fine spray spurted from the muzzle of his gun, to become a vaporous cloud about the saboteurs' heads. The spies collapsed like two ripped meal-bags, thudded to the ground, lay motionless.

AT ONCE the counter-spy leaped into furious action. His lithe figure sprang forward, in an instant he had heaved the unconscious saboteurs into their tiny craft, and shoved it off and whipped into it. He let it slide out into the Sound with the momentum of his initial shove, let the current take it. The fog closed around the boat. There was a dull plop into the water, then a second. Those particular bombs would lie at the bottom of the East River till Judgment Day. A tiny, hooded light flickered over a swarthy face; touched ascetic lips, a close-trimmed, black mustache; went out. A black cloak fluttered overside, a gray mask followed....

Minutes later a limp body, clad only in shirt and drawers, bulked along the rowboat's gunwale. "God take your soul, Dominic Liscio. You did your duty as you saw it."

The river chuckled gruesomely as it clasped yet another flaccid bundle to its muddy bosom. Then muffled oars dipped softly into the stream and the boat's bow turned toward the loom of the *Santa Maria*, until the rowboat reached and thudded against its rust-streaked hull.

From the deck of the tramp steamer a cautious voice called, in Italian, "Who is it?"

"Liscio," the whispered reply came in perfect Piedmontese,

and in the voice of the man whose corpse now bobbed somewhere on the Sound's scummed flood. "Dominic Liscio. Get us on board quickly. Angelo has met with an accident, he's unconscious. Help me with him."

An unintelligible exclamation came from above, feet thudded. The man in the boat heard an authoritative rumble, curiously guttural for an officer of an Italian vessel. Then a Jacob's ladder coiled down, and he had fastened the boat to its end, had lifted Angelo to reaching hands, toward a flashlight's glare above, and was himself stepping on to the dim deck.

Shadowy forms were barely visible. One approached, broad-shouldered, paunchy, the shape of his head unmistakably Teutonic. Light flicked over the figure standing there in Dominic Liscio's clothes, and fingering Dominic Liscio's close-clipped black mustache so that his hand all but screened a swarthy face that might have been Liscio's own. "Well, what happened?"

Liscio's reincarnation responded in English, taking the cue. "We got the bombs planted, all right. Hell will break loose in half an hour. We'd better get away from here. Someone—"

"Wait. Tell me in the cabin. Come." The other turned, waddled on thick legs to a companionway. Warm light irradiated the mist as a door opened, fanned out. The disguised Red Finger's eyes slid to a face just revealed at the edge of the luminance; his lids narrowed. But he followed the German into the cabin and the door shut behind him.

HE STOOD just within that door, watching his bulky shaven-polled host, and his fingers hovered near the lapel of Liscio's pea-jacket. The other heaved around, his flabby cheeks quivered. He was just beyond a table on which were a pitcher and a tall glass on the inside of which yellow foam still made dripping rings. His hamlike arms hung straight down and his hands were concealed by the edge of the table. "Now we can speak with more comfort. Tell me about it."

"First you tell me something, Herr Gans. Tell me how it happens that a Nazi spy is serving in the Italian Secret Service?"

The vast expanse of Gans' face was expressionless, but his piglike eyes glittered. "Ach! Once more! I told already that I was unjustly cashiered by von Goering when I reported that I had killed that dangerous American, Red Finger, and afterwards it was proved I was mistaken. Why must you ask that question again?"

"Because it just occurred to me that if our little expedition had been tipped-off to the Americans and they had captured two obvious Italians sabotaging their gas-mask plant, this country would have been swept by a tempest of rage that would have forced its leaders to throw the power of the United States on the side of Hitler in the coming struggle."

The German's red mouth twisted. "True. But what of it? They were not tipped-off."

The other's voice dropped a note, was thick with menace. "But they were, Herr Gans. They were. And I think that fact will be of great interest to my compatriots aboard." He half-twisted, got a hand on the doorknob, then froze, held for an instant by a sudden sound over his shoulder.

"Stop!" Gans barked. "Stop—*Red Finger!*"

The American's eyes flicked back, saw the black tunnel-mouth of a forty-five automatic snouting at him. He came fully around to face that menace, his hands went above his head, and he smiled.

"Good, Herr Gans! Very good! Suspecting my imposture you got me in here and you had that gun ready to flash on me at the proper time. But how did you know?"

"Liscio was provided with a password to use when he returned, though I knew he would not return. When you did not use it, I knew you were not him. And who else could you be but—Red Finger? Only you, Red Finger, would have defeated the plan to wreck the gas-mask plant without the repercussion on which I counted, and then have the skill and the nerve to come here made up as the man you have killed."

"Thanks for the compliment." The counter-spy, at the mercy of his archenemy, appeared as carefree as though the table between them were set for a luncheon instead of being spread for death. "But I must return it. Your whole scheme was clever, too clever, in fact for you to have evolved it." The German's smirk was suddenly replaced by a black scowl. "May I venture to guess that it was suggested to you by—a certain Baron Odun, that suave, brilliant chief-spy of—an Asiatic power."

The fury that leaped into the other's pink face rendered verbal admission unnecessary. The American's eyebrows arched, and he went smoothly on. "Perhaps it did not occur to you that he was making you a catspaw to pull his country's chestnuts out of the fire?"

"A catspaw," the Nazi spluttered. "Ach! What nonsense. How a catspaw?"

"Simply enough. With all Europe at each other's throats, and the United States embroiled, how simple it would be for that Far Eastern empire to wait till the nations of the white race were bled white and then strike—surely, swiftly, with certainty of success. Our Pacific Coast stripped of its man-power, our fleet concentrated in the Atlantic…. You see? In a week Odun's country would be entrenched in North America, and then—world domination!"

Fear flickered Gans' pig-eyes. Then they glazed over with red hate. "You talk well, Red Finger. But it will not save you. I shall not miss this time." His fat finger trembled on the trigger. "You die—now!"

The American's long leg darted out, thudded against the underside of the cabin table. It lifted, crashed against Gans' rotund belly. The pistol crashed; the shot thudded into wood. Red Finger was a streak of black action as he hurtled across the room.

A knife flashed in yellow light from beyond Red Finger's shoulder, and its gleam was quenched in fat flesh. Blood spurted from a thick neck, but, uncannily, the crimson blood seemed to catch only one finger of the counter-spy, the trigger finger of his right hand, dyed that finger scarlet.

"**VERY GOOD**," an oily voice slid into the room. "I could not have done better myself. The American gasped, lifted to his feet.

A slender, saturnine sailor was inside the closed door, the

faintest of smiles twisting his tight lips. "But don't try anything like that on me." The hands that held two flat automatics were long-fingered, almost effeminate; their skin was oddly tinged, and the crescents at the base of their queerly pointed nails were deeply blue, strangely exotic.

"Odun!" Red Finger said quietly. "I might have guessed you'd be here!"

"Unfortunately—for you—I came to the same conclusion as he did, from the same premises. And Red Finger has put too many spokes into my wheels for me to miss this opportunity to dispose of him once and for all." Except for an almost imperceptible odd hiss the man's English was precise, even stilted. "I regret exceedingly the necessity of terminating the life of so gallant an adversary."

Under the film of brown with which he had painted it Red Finger's face was gray, drawn with defeat. "So you win at last, Odun! But I wonder if you would grant me a favor."

The characteristic round eyes of his race in the saffron face were wary. But Odun's tone was courteous, almost regretful. "If I can, but..." he shrugged, deprecatingly. "I shall not take any chances with you. You can hardly blame me." He nodded to the quivering, jellylike mass that had once been the ace of the Nazi secret agents.

"All I want is a puff at one last cigarette—yours if you wish."

Odun's usually impassive countenance showed just a trace of puzzlement, but his racial code of courtesy forbade refusal, as Red Finger well knew. "I have none," he said, "but you may take out and light your own, if you give me your word you will not draw a weapon instead."

"Thank you," the American responded gravely. "I do give my word." Then, at Odun's nod, his hand slipped into a pocket, came out with a package of cigarettes and a lighter. The white tube in his mouth, a little flame flared at the quick rasp of his thumb and he inhaled gratefully. "You know," he said. "If America did nothing else for the world her gift of tobacco entitles Columbus to immortality."

"But you must admit that it was the East that brought that gift to its perfection. Just so, when Asia conquers the world, we of the East will make it a far better place in which to live, even for you whites."

Red Finger's cigarette glowed redly. "That will be—"

With the last word a sudden puff sent the cigarette flying across space into Odun's eyes. The arch-spy's instinctive gesture to avoid it was uncontrollable, and Red Finger seized that split second to catapult upon him.

His fists flailed, so fast that they were a mere blur, the spats of their landing a single sound. Odun crashed against the bulkhead, Red Finger twisted, had the door open and was through it and over the rail before the startled seamen outside realized that the door was open. Someone shouted; muddy water geysered; and the fog and the night closed their impenetrable veil over the muddy water.

A SKULKING figure found an alley between two houses on Thirteenth Street in the block between Third and Fourth Avenues, and vanished into its shadows. That same figure might have been seen, had there been anyone to look, wearily climbing a fire-escape ladder to a roof, flitting shadow-like over gravelled tin, vanishing into the square, dawn-cast shadow of a brick chimney. But when the sun's beams filtered across that roof, minutes later, no human form marked its blank expanse.

Six stories below, the ceiling of Ford Duane's secret cubicle opened like a trapdoor, and the bookseller's weary form dropped through. The hook-lined wall open, shut again. And a perennially weary, young-old man touched flame to his breakfast gas-stove....

The web holding the Scythe of Death from its disastrous fall seemed a trifle stronger this morning. But the two grim sentinels still held their place at each doorpost of Ford Duane's Second-hand Bookstore.

RED FINGER—DEATH DEALER

THE SKY was a bleak, gray vault over the city, sifting down a fine mist of chill rain. Along Fourth Avenue, the rows of bookstalls were tarpaulin-covered, and muddy rivulets streaked the window of Duane's Second-Hand Bookstore. Within, lank and drooping-lidded, Ford Duane moved noiselessly between the gloom-shrouded, high walls of weary volumes across whose backs his fingers whispered lovingly. A single carbon lamp, pendant from an encrusted cord, spread heavy shadows on the bare boards of the floor and on the book-filled shelving—shadows that were somehow darkly alive and pregnant with an odd menace.

Veiled as they were, the eyes of the long-legged bookseller were keenly blue, strangely restless. They flecked about constantly with a wariness wholly at variance with the drowsy peace of the deserted shop; and under his stained alpaca smock, tense muscles quivered with readiness for instant action. The thud of a passing footfall, the creak of a drying beam, twitched his sharp ascetic face to them and tightened his thin lips, time and again, till their source, their innocence, had been established.

The doorknob rattled and Duane whirled to the sound, his hand flashing to an inner pocket. A ragged, swarthy man scraped sodden shoes on the threshold and smiled ingratiatingly. "Please," he said in the liquid accents of southern Italy. "Please

attend to moosic, meester." He gestured vaguely with a battered flute clutched in one dirty, gnarled hand. "Pay all that you like."

Duane relaxed, but his face was rigid, expressionless. "No. No, I have work to do." He crossed, with his curiously silent glide, to a paint-peeled writing table near the door and slid into its broken chair. "And I have no money." He pulled a sheet of yellow paper toward him, a pencil. "I'll be playing in the street myself if business keeps up the way it is. Try next door."

The musician did not stir. But Duane seemed to have utterly forgotten the intrusion. He frowned musingly, and inscribed three letters at the head of the sheet. P-A-T. A gleam flickered in the beggar's eyes, vanished. He shrugged, back into the street.

Duane smiled, fleetingly and without humor. He drew five horizontal lines across the paper, the five lines of the musical staff—and held his pencil poised, as if waiting for inspiration. But his eyes wandered to the three letters he had written, and his thin lips moved, repeating the flutist's words; *"Please attend to moosic. Pay all that you like."* Was it only coincidence that the initial letters of the first three words of each sentence were the same, and were identical with those he had jotted down?

A flurry of heavier rain beat at the window. Its tattoo seemed like fingers rapping a message on the glass, a message of death. P-A-T! Once an old man had sold Duane a dog-eared volume he represented as a *P*etronius, printed by *A*rden and bound by *T*rant. That night, men had died, suddenly, mysteriously. On another occasion, a pushcart hawker had called his wares, *"P*ails! *A*xes! *T*eenvare! The bookdealer had made a purchase from him, and when the sun visited the city again, two bloated corpses were bobbing on the greasy waters of Long Island Sound. Now once more the three ominous letters had prefaced apparently innocuous words where Ford could hear them....

Shrill sound pierced the wall separating Duane from the store next door, the lilting rhythm of a popular song. *"Have you ever seen a dream walking?"* the flute asked, muted by the intervening, thin partition. But the sugary flow of the tune was sprayed by a spatter of grace notes dropped in by awkward fingers fumbling the instrument's stops. The discordance rambled through the melody, flew as it jotted down—*those very notes!* "—*the Heaven in my arms was you.*" The flute sobbed into silence. The five horizontal lines on Ford's paper were filled now by the hieroglyphics of musical shorthand. The thin-faced man looked at the sheet before him:

He paused a moment, considered the arrangement of the notes he had written, and suddenly his pencil was moving again, setting down English letters over the music he had inscribed:

"Odon at Kensico since Sun. Why? T."

FORD DUANE stared long at the paper on the desk before him, while lumping muscles ridge his lean jaw and a veil seems to drop across his eyes. The fingers of the rain tap against the storefront, but he hears only the fingers of Death rapping on his door. Not for him. This seeming shopkeeper has lived and breathed in the tangible presence of danger too long to fear it. The threat whose icy breath chills him is for the unsuspecting people of the teeming human warren called New York, for the women and the little children. At Kensico, in Westchester, the metropolis drinking water bids farewell to the sun before it plunges underground into great mains that divide and subdivide till their final capillaries reach into the city's multifarious homes and gush the fluid of life into glasses, pots, and infants' feeding bottles. At Kensico, if anywhere, is the City's vulnerable point, the Achilles' heel where an enemy may strike once, and slay a million-fold.

But we have no enemy—America is at peace with all the world. Duane's lax hand lies on a newspaper, today's *Times*. On an inside page, a small item notes that the transfer of gold from the San Francisco mint to mid-continent safety has been completed. Safety from what? Earthquakes, the treasury says. But the San Francisco Mint withstood the 1905 cataclysm with not a crack in its walls.

Yesterday the guard on the Panama Canal was doubled. Was that also to guard against earthquakes? For two years the fleet has been concentrated in the Pacific, while shipyards all over the country ring with feverish building. Earthquakes again?

In a far-off oriental land, men with reptilian eyes and tinted skin drink silent toasts to the Day when the red sun of the island empire shall dye the Occidental World with the lurid stain of the White Race's ultimate blood. Europe is torn with internal strife, bled white by its own vampire politicians, already an easy prey to saffron hordes ready to overrun it—did not America bar the way. America! Still strong! Still stalwart!

America must be weakened or dreams of World Domination will never be realized. America must be weakened—by strikes, by disease, by calamities mysteriously propagated and mysteriously spread. It is not the people of that distant land who have so decreed; it is not their King. Nevertheless someone has proclaimed America's destruction, and the rats dispatched to the task scutter in the darkness, gnawing, gnawing, gnawing....

Night-dark deepens in the drizzling street. Ford Duane sighs, lifts from his seat, locks his store-door, clicks out the one hanging light. He is like a gray ghost, slithering back to the curtained alcove in the rear where a frowsy cot, a table cluttered by unwashed dishes, and a single gas-plate on an up-ended box are all the home he has. He is like a phantom—and suddenly has vanished.

A keen eye might have noted the flicker of movement that was the swift raising and lowering of a trapdoor whose edges are so skillfully fashioned that now they cannot be discerned. A keen ear might have noted, momentarily, the scraping of fabric against stone beneath the bookstore. A ferret is prowling the underground burrows of the yellow rats that gnaw....

THE CLOUDS have dispersed. There is a moon this midnight, and under the loom of Kensico Dam a hundred cars are parked while lovers whisper or are dreamily silent. Above them hangs a million watery tons of life and death, restrained by a staunch wall of stone. Above them creeps a more deadly peril, and one man alone can guard them from it.

Two miles north of the dam, the billowing dark blanket of the woods folds close to the silver sheet of the man-created lake. Here there are no cars, no whispering lovers. The sylvan silence is broken only by the ripple of breeze-stroked water and the piercing hymn of a myriad insects of the night. Solitude, primordial quiet, reign supreme here, a half-hour from the tumult of

Times Square—the peace of green and growing things. Peace—abruptly the insect-piping is silenced; the woods seem to listen with bated breath. Underbrush rustles and a shadowy form emerges from the trees.

An arrow of light darts across the lake's surface, spatters against the shore. The moon's effulgence takes the intruder. He is squat, stocky. The sleek, black hair of his hatless head lies close to the skull. Cold cruelty glitters in his black, perfectly round eyes and tightens his fleshless lips to a straight gash across his oddly tinted face. Even his walk, as he slithers across the narrow band of pebbles to the water's edge, is somehow exotic, somehow—reptilian.

He stands motionless, gazing across the reservoir, gazing at the pale glow of the southern horizon beneath which the city spreads. His arm hangs straight down at his side; in its hand is a small, black satchel circled by thick straps. That hand is long-fingered, almost effeminate. Its nails are filed to sharp points and the crescents at their bases are deeply, queerly blue. There is about this man an aura of evil, of chill malevolence from which the very trees seem to shudder away.

The Oriental kneels, places his black bag on the ground. His hands move deftly, the straps fall away, there is the click of a lock and the bag is open. He fumbles within, brings out a long, thick cylinder of glass within which a viscous transparent liquid absorbs the moon's silver and turns it to a green radiance eerily suggestive of putrescence—of rotting, plague-stricken cadavers.

The man smiles, slowly, satanically, and he tugs at the cotton-swathed cork plugging the tube of death. The pop as it comes free is startlingly loud in the stillness. He twists to spill the green liquid into the water from which New York will drink tomorrow.

A cold, grim voice sounds abruptly from the tree-shadows. "Hold it! *Hold it just that way, Baron Odon.*"

Something in that sudden voice freezes the *saboteur* as if he has been sprayed by a jet of dry ice. Only a sharp hiss of startled breath shows that he is alive.

Again the underbrush rustles with human movement. A shadow firms, slides out on the tiny beach. It is a tall figure of darkness in the moonlight, a shapeless blue detached from the velvet night. Odon, cringing on his knees, the lethal container in one hand and its stopper in the other, glimpses a concealing black robe, topped by a shapeless gray felt and a gray mask from behind whose twin slits menace glints. His fear-widened eyes fasten on the muzzle of a revolver snouting pointblank at him, on a revolver and on the rock-steady hand gripping its butt.

That hand is a blob of black, almost invisible against the cloak's blackness. But one finger, the finger that curls about the gun's trigger, is blood-red, a dash of scarlet weirdly awesome. The Asiatic's lips twitch, soundlessly form a name. "Red Finger!"

IN THE dark subterranean world where the silent, eternal war is waged that waits for no ultimatums, no booming drums nor blaring bugles, that name is one of dread. More than one master-spy has been erased from the lists of his nation by that scarlet digit, more than one fine-wrought scheme for America's destruction has been smashed by him whose badge it is. In a dozen chancelleries, a fortune waits to reward him who can prove that Red Finger no longer lives…. "Put that cork back into the tube, firmly." The words drip from under the speaker's gray mask, each a slow syllable of infinite threat.

Odon obeys. Death is once more stoppered. "Stand up and hand it to me."

The Oriental comes lithely erect, holds out the green cylinder at arm's length. Red Finger's other hand, black-gloved, appears from the folds of his cloak to take it. Something whips from the murk of the woods, close behind him—something thin and snakelike. It coils about his neck, tightens. Odon drops to the sand, just under a spray of fine mist that jets from the counter-spy's gun. The American jerks back, gurgling, clawing at the thing that has clamped off his breath, that is dragging him irresistibly backward. Yellow hands clutch Red Finger's ankles; he crashes to the ground. Odon is swarming over him, wrests the gun from his grip, coils and knots a long, strong cord about the American's wrists and his ankles. Quick, uncouth words crackle from his lips and a third form of mystery comes out of the shadows, chuckling.

"Checkmate this time, my dear Red Finger," the Asiatic pants, as he loosens the garroting filament from the other's neck and rises to look gloatingly down at his helpless adversary. A gray mask dangles from his long fingers. "Or shall I call you—Ford Duane, dealer in second-hand books?" His utterance is clipped, precise, only that odd hiss reveals that he is using an alien tongue.

Duane, arms and legs lashed, weaponless, in the power of his implacable enemy, looked up and smiled. "My felicitations, Baron Odon." His blue eyes, murky now with defeat and despair, peered past the Asiatic to the other, the one who had so skillfully garroted him in the very moment of his seeming victory. He saw a swarthy, Italianate face; thick lips twisted in a grin that still had something of the ingratiating quality of the psuedo-beggar's smile, the beggar whose flute had skirled a cryptic invitation to die. "You fooled me neatly."

Odon bowed with the exaggerated politeness of oriental etiquette. "Not any more neatly than you have fooled me, so many times. But you were handicapped by the inferiority of your race. When I made up my mind to concentrate upon removing you it was impossible for me to fail."

Except for his eyes, the counter-spy's countenance revealed only interest in the master-stroke of a skilled antagonist. "How did you manage it? Only T knew who I was. He was always himself the messenger, and we used a different code each time."

"Your scheme had a fatal weakness. T is the head of your Intelligence Service. Others as well as you report to him and they are not all as skillful. I detected one, fed him information, watched him till he slipped once in communicating with your Chief. Then T himself came under my scrutiny—the rest was easy."

Red Finger shrugged. "Well, you win, Odon. This time. But there are others, always there will be others till *you* slip in your turn. We do not live long, we who fight the invisible war."

"No," the oriental's voice was very low. "We do not live long, and no tears are shed when we die. But tears are shed while we live, many tears. Look!" He stooped. When he rose, the tube of green death was again in his hand, open. "You die tonight;

tomorrow there will be mourning in your nation. But not for you, my friend, not for you alone." His arm snapped, whiplike. An emerald stream arced through the moonshine, splashed into the reservoir, was gone. "The stuff is heavy, Duane, it sinks to the bottom where the currents are swift. In an hour it will be in the mains, by morning a hundred thousand housewives will sniff a faint odor in their cooking and wonder whether they have failed to clean their pots well enough. By night.... Wherever you are by tonight you will be welcoming others, many others to those Golden Streets of which your priests prate."

DUANE'S FACE was white against the silver sands, white even to the lips, but his eyes blazed fury. "You fiend!" he gritted. "You unspeakable thing! God—your God and mine—will damn you forever for that!"

Odon's smile was blind. "My God will reward me with the sight of streets strewn with the corpses of white-faced menials who make way for the inheritors of His earth.... But I have no more time for you.... Tony—the knife!"

The swart renegade to his race stepped forward, a blade glittered bluely as he bent, caught the light as it swept down, straight to Duane's bared throat. The American was suddenly doubled up in a jack-knife. Folding almost too swift for the eye to follow, his bound legs lashed out, his heels plunked into the stabber's groin. An agonized shriek split the silence, the Italian lifted to the tremendous impetus of that unexpected, two-heeled kick, catapulted across the strand and writhed, prostrate on the beach.

Duane was rolling, his new motion continuous with that which had laid the Italian low, toward the startled Oriental.

Before Odon quite realized what had happened, Ford thudded against his legs. The Asiatic toppled, his hand flashing to a pocket even as he fell, coming out with a flat, black automatic. A shot blazed orange flame into sand. Duane flipped a back-somersault, came incredibly to his feet for an instant, hurled himself headfirst at Odon. Another shot spat flatly, pounded sickeningly into flesh. Ford's skull thumped against Odon's chin. He whipped about and his teeth were sunk into the other's gun hand. Blood spurted over his lips; his head twisted, bone snapped and the automatic span away across pebbles, plopped into water.

Odon's left arm came up and over Duane's shoulder, long yellow fingers slid along Ford's neck, searching for that spot behind the ear where life comes near the surface, at the mercy of a probing thumb. The maelstrom of combat split as Duane whirled away from the fatal jab. Again he launched into a flashing backward flip that brought him erect, bound as he was. His knees bent, his thigh muscles exploded, and he was leaping, almost flying, through the air. His heels crashed against Odon's chest, he jarred down on his spine, whirled over to meet his antagonist.

And lay still, gasping for breath, as he saw that the Asiatic was quite motionless at the water's edge, his thin, cruel lips edged by a red foam.

A hot iron bored into Duane's shoulder, where Odon's bullet had struck. His body was one huge ache and his lungs felt as though flames seared them. Blood dribbled from cuts at his wrists, at his ankles, where the cords had cut deep during the almost miraculous acrobatics by which he, even though tightly bound, had vanquished two armed men. Ford's smoldering glance sought the other, the Italian who would have knifed him at the command of the spy. He was gone. He must have run away as soon as the first paralyzing effect of the blow he had received had passed. Well, hirelings are rarely faithful. But he had left his knife, there at the water's edge. After awhile, Duane thought dazedly, he could crawl to that knife and get free.

Then Red Finger saw a thick glass cylinder half-buried in the sand, empty now except for a few green drops that still clung to its lips. He groaned. That emerald liquid was at the bottom of the reservoir, being carried slowly toward the huge pipes that would split, and split again till their final branching would bring death into the very homes of New York's millions. An hour, Odon had said. An hour! How long was it since then? How much time was there left?

THE PARKED cars were gone from the huge plaza below Kensico Dam. It was late, very late, and in the stone gatehouse atop the great wall Tim O'Hara drowsed in his cushioned chair and thought of the corned-beef and cabbage Kitty would have ready for him when he got home in the morning. This was a cushy job, he thought, watching those big valves that could shut-off the water from the city at a click-over of this switch that was wide across as a man's head. Made a man feel like somebody, knowing he could make a big city thirsty just by a twist of his wrist. Not that Tim had ever had occasion to click the switch in the five years since the boss had got him the job, nor he wouldn't in five more years. But he could if he wanted to....

Tim O'Hara rubbed his eyes and settled lower on his spine. Time for forty winks before he had to go-around with his oil-squirter and bit of waste. *What was that?*

Running feet thudded on stone outside. Someone was pounding on the big oak door that shut out the curious from the gate-house. "Open up!" a muffled voice came through the wood. "Open up in there!"

Tim got heavily to his feet. "Who is it?" he called. "Who wants in?"

"Open, damn you!" The fellow, whoever he was, was mush-mouthed for all his yelling. Some drunk from Valhalla, mebbe, raising hell. Well, Tim would put a flea in his ear and send him away damn quick. The gate-tender picked up a huge spanner, limbered across the concrete floor under the tremendous gleaming circles of the hand-wheels that could be used to raise or lower the gates to the big mains if for some reason the motors did not function. He got to the door, got his hand on its knob, swung the portal open.

"What the hell—," he began, and stopped, open-mouthed at the spectacle that presented itself. The head of the man outside lolled against the door sash to which he clung with clack-gloved hands that were muddy, ripped. His face was scratched, streaked by dried blood. His eyes were half-shut and what could be seen of them was a bleary red. Some black rags hung from his shoulders, his wrists were swollen to twice their size. One shoe was gone entirely, the other blood-clotted. A green vine was twisted, queerly exuberant, around his waist. One does not crash at top speed through two miles of lightless underbrush and brambles with impunity.

Duane looked dazedly at Tim's florid face. He mumbled something unintelligible, pushed himself away from the lintel. "Shut—shut off the water!"

O'Hara took a backward step, lifting his spanner. The man wasn't drunk; he was stark, staring crazy. "Git away from here," he grunted. "Before I crack you."

Ford's mouth twisted. "Listen, man. There's poison in the reservoir. Poison!"

Tim spat on a calloused palm, took a firmer grip on his wrench. "Poison is it? Oi'll poison yuhr skull to a pulp if you don't beat it quick's your tootsies'll take you."

The counter-spy's glance slid over O'Hara's bulking shoulder, saw a clock against the wall. Its hands made a narrow V at the top of the dial. One o'clock. The hour was up, or almost so. "Oh God! Will you show some sense? Half New York will die tomorrow if you don't throw the switch at once."

"There's one guy thot's goin' to wish he' dead in about tin seconds," O'Hara bellowed, and lunged at the intruder. The spanner whistled through the air, crashed against the doorpost as Duane dipped in a sudden crouch. He came up within the long, simian arms of the gateman, came up with his fist flailing. Smack! It caught O'Hara flush on the button. Tim's eyes glazed, he reeled, dropped.

DUANE SHOOK his own head to clear away the gray mists welling up in his tired brain, shuffled into the station. A vertical slab of bluish stone was studded with bare-poled switches. At its very center, the biggest pair of copper studs was neatly labelled: OPEN-MAIN-MOTORS-SHUT. It took every ounce of energy he had left to stagger to the switchboard, to get his fingers around the black handle of that biggest switch and pull it down, thrust it home.

A dim hum, somewhere beneath the floor, rose to a roar. The building vibrated to the whirling of gigantic armatures, laboring to close down the watergates, to shut-off the poisoned water from the people twenty miles away.

He must rest now... rest....

Then he heard leather tap on stone at the door behind him! Odon's squat form, his blood-smeared, yellow countenance was framed in the doorway, the leveled automatic in the Asiatic's left hand.

Duane put his own hand out, found the back of Tim's chair, held himself erect by holding on to it. Below his feet a muffled, enormous thud pounded, and the motor-hum stopped. "You're too late, Odon," he said. "The water's shut off."

There was no humor in the spy's thinlipped smile. "It can be turned on again." He slithered softly across the floor, edging toward the switchboard, pivoting around the black muzzle of his gun that was fixed unwaveringly on Duane's belly. His right hand was twisted, brown with blood, but it lifted behind him, lifted unerringly to the handle of the main switch, tugged to bring it over, to open the gates to the green death. Blue lightning crackled as copper bars pulled out of the studs marked: SHUT, as the switch wheeled over to enter those marked: OPEN....

And Duane's arm swept up. The gatekeeper's chair came up

with it, hurtled across the narrow space between spy and counter-spy, crashed against the Asiatics head, crashed it against the switch.

A thousand volts of blue lightning fizzed, crackled, roared through human flesh. Black smoke misted the light in the gate-house, and the acrid aroma of charred meat was pungent in the little chamber. That which had been Hayashura Odon, Baron of a distant Eastern nation, master *saboteur*, pitched to the floor.

Ford Duane staggered, retched with nausea, and tumbled atop him. But in the gate-house on Kensico Dam, the motors did not roar again. And when the police that O'Hara would call should come and arouse Red Finger, certain muttered words, the furtive showing of a secret sign, would set him free to dive into his lair once more, there to lick his wounds against the time when again his country should have need of him.

CAGED HORROR

LONG-LIMBED, GAWKY, Ford Duane leaned against the dust-filmed doorjamb of his second-hand bookshop and blinked sleepily out at Fourth Avenue, asphalt-paved and deserted. Elsewhere New York was just awakening to its hectic evening of pleasure, but here the day was ended and the yellow glimmer of the storelight behind him was a futile gesture at inviting trade. Passersby now would be too few and too hurried to browse among Duane's musty shelves.

Yet, as a man's figure was silhouetted against a corner street lamp's blue-white cone, Ford's young-old face seemed almost imperceptibly to tighten, and the narrow slit of his eyes seemed to glimmer with a queer expectancy. An odd readiness for instantaneous action quivered in his gaunt body like a leashed spring. It was as if some inner alarm suddenly had been set off. As if Ford Duane had heard the rattle of Death startlingly along this dormant street.

Now the distant form pounds purposefully along the sidewalk, comes opposite Duane's vantage point, pauses. Ford can see now that the man has a pipe in his mouth, that he is fumbling in a pocket of his topcoat, evidently for a match. He finds and strikes one, lifts it to the pipe bowl.

The tiny spark flares up; vanishes as the stranger pulls the flame into the tobacco he is igniting; flares again, vanishes once more. Queerly the little spurts of light seem to make a pattern of dots and dashes—the flashing letters of the Continental Code! P - A - T. And again P - A - T. Then the match is flicked away, and the smoker starts off once more on his interrupted progress toward a subway kiosk.

But the bookman, blue eyes aglow with a strange light, shoots a quick glance up and down the empty street, and shifts his position, lifting a long, angular arm to rest a hand on the doorjamb above his head. Those three letters, of all the alphabet's twenty-six, have time and again come to this somnolent bookshop and its languorous owner. And each time those letters came men have died, obscure soldiers in the underground war of spy against counter-spy, of saboteur against secret service agent, that never ends.

For a nation's existence depends on the secret, perilous labors of unsung heroes like Ford Duane; upon men like the nameless messenger who, getting Duane's signal that the coast is clear, turns at the next corner to cross Fourth Avenue and deliver whatever it is he has for the undercover ace. Something of extreme importance it must be, that it is being brought so openly. Little muscles make a lumping ridge along the pseudo-shopkeeper's gaunt jaw. The blood pulses more warmly in his veins, sings in his ears....

But that sound is *not* the blood in his ears. It is the sudden, shrill hum of a buzzing gas engine. A motorcycle flashes out from the sidestreet where the courier is crossing, skids around, strikes the man squarely. He arcs, a limp, sprawling figure, high in the air; thuds down head first, sickeningly. The motorcycle sputters a machine-gun-like protest at the collision; weaves drunkenly about, its goggle-masked rider fighting to control it. And before Duane can start his frantic dash the murder-machine has straightened, is hurtling away, arrowlike down the long dim reach of the Avenue, its roar fading out in the dull grumble of the unknowing city.

Ford pounds toward the flaccid dark heap in the gutter. If there is thought at all in his frozen brain at that moment it is that his unknown colleague may be dead, but that the message has not been touched, that it is still waiting for him. *Unless it was verbal*—unless it is locked forever in a silenced brain!

He drops to his knees beside that pitiful, broken heap, staring into the blanched face which is turned sightlessly toward him, and from mouth and nose smears of vivid scarlet tell their own tale. But it is the crushed-in skull that finishes any slight hope Duane might have that his comrade may still be alive. Ford's long, pallid fingers search swiftly through pockets, through the various secret interstices of the courier's daubed, torn, gore-clotted clothing. Nothing!

The undercover man rocks back on his heels. That, then, is why the murderer did not stop to search his victim!

A VIBRATION, an almost unheard footfall, the sixth sense those gain who walk always with danger, *something*, jerks Duane around, heaves him erect in a single lithe movement. Just in time! A shadow grows, changes into a man's shape, and hurtles at him. Ford glimpses the flicker of a drawn knife sweeping thirstily for his throat, glimpses a high-cheekboned, saffron face. His fist smashes that face and bone crunches under the

steelknuckled impact. His left arm launches another pile-driver blow, and the assailant lifts on the end of the white man's arm. His weapon spirals away, clatters into darkness. The Mongolian sinks down alongside the dead American.

Duane's countenance is now a marble mask, expressionless but somehow dread-inspiring as the visage of a basilisk. A pulse throbs in each temple, and his pupils are tiny, feral. Not many who have seen his features so transformed have lived to remember it. And yet, somehow, he seems puzzled.

The knifer's open attack on him was unnatural, not consistent with the usual tactics of under-cover combat. If They had penetrated his disguise as an innocuous vender of old books, then They would have found some more subtle way to encompass his destruction. The assault must have been inspired by some other motive. For what other reason than to dispose of an interloper who interfered with the recovery of something for which this other agent had been slain?

But there isn't anything on the corpse, not where it could have been gotten at quickly and transmitted with a minimum risk of discovery. The poor fellow had been almost at his goal, would have had the missive at his fingertips....

At his fingertips! Involuntarily Duane glances to the dead hands, at the pipe that is still held in the left, at the fingers of the right hand, fastened so curiously over the bowl. Duane's tight lips twitch; he pulls the pipe gently from between those stiffening fingers.

The briar is still warm, the blackened flakes it cups are still smoldering.... And from the left, heavy approaching footfalls thump.

Duane thrusts the pipe into his own pocket, brings his hand out with a small metal cylinder that goes to his lips. The sound of his breath evokes the piercing, blood-exciting shrillness of a police whistle. It seems to echo from out of the dark canyon of sleeping lofts and office buildings. Then a big-shouldered, blue-uniformed patrolman pounds into sight, running....

THE FRONT door of Duane's Secondhand Bookshop was locked now, the volume-filled shelves behind it abandoned to black, dust-smelling darkness. In the rear of the long store, behind curtains slung over a sagging pole, Ford Duane sat on his creaking cot and looked drearily at the gnarled, large-bowled pipe.

He rapped out black ashes, a wet dottle, onto the floor, peered into the receptacle whence they came. There was only char within, and the single hole at the bottom through which smoke might enter the stem. Duane thrust his thumb into the bowl, hooked it and twisted. The inside of the bowl made a quarter turn, slid out of the shell within which it was contained.

The undercover man grunted with satisfaction. The inner bowl still thimble-like on his thumb, he poked a little finger into the place where it had been, fished out a folded bit of thin paper. He grunted in admiration. It was not only a good hiding place, but if a man was captured, a twist of that bowl while the pipe being smoked would burn up any incriminating evidence.

Then he was unfolding the message and squinted in amazement to find it in clear English, not in any of the many ingenious codes used by the Service of which he was a part. *Haste!* Desperate haste. Time to encipher, to decode the epistle was lacking; it must be written, delivered, read in desperate haste.

And acted then in greater haste than even the writer could have known. The corpse that would lie in the Morgue for weeks, and finally find an unnamed grave was in itself a sufficient warning.

A HUGE ocean liner warped into its pier. In the great, flood-lighted shed, trunks, valises, gaudily labelled grips were being piled around columns bearing placard letters, and their anxious-eyed owners were seeking them out, keys in hand. Seeking them out also were jutting-jawed men in peaked caps and blue uniforms—Uncle Sam's Customs inspectors.

A hand-truck, piled high with luggage, rumbled down a gangplank but did not stop at any of the lettered pillars. It rolled straight down the long concrete passage to the big iron gates at the pier-front, and the guard there swung those gates open for it. Black letters on a white ground, pasted on the three big trunks that the truck carried, explained its privilege of free passage:

Diplomatic Baggage

So these three trunks are passed out, quite uninspected, to the broad, cobbled expanse of West Street. And, following the loaded truck a short, wiry individual whose black eyes were slanted in a tinted, emotionless countenance, but who was as dapper as any other rising young diplomat, cat-footed silently out of shadows between the *Apgaria's* pier and that next to it.

The stalwart deckhand who brought the hand truck thus far tipped the device dexterously, so that the trunks slid off with a minimum of jar. He turns to the Oriental. "Needn't tell me ter be careful, sir. I could 'ear they was somefin bloody well aloive in that top box."

The other's lips moved in a smile, but his eyes were somehow narrower, colder than before. "You are mithtaken," he lisped. "Oh, quite mithtaken." He thrust a slim hand at the seaman; a crisp, green bill passed from it to the cockney's capacious paw.

"Thankee, Sir. Guess I was a bit h'off thinkin' I 'eard a scutterin' an' athumpin' as I come along."

"Yeth, you were," the diplomat sighed. "By the way, would

you mind thtepping down to that thecond pier from here and telling my man I am ready for him?"

The deckhand took another look at the banknote, has seen the numeral in its corner, and he became all obsequiousness. "Yes, sir. Of course, sir."

The Englishman starts off to the left, darkness swallows him. The yellow man made a peculiar gesture; a motorcycle pudded softly out of dimness to the right and stopped briefly beside the three trunks. One handlebar seemed a trifle askew, and there was a red stain at the front wheel's fork. The haunched-over, goggle-masked rider listens to a few swift words from the almond-eyed man, then slid away after the seaman who has talked too much.

Almost immediately after that a small black Ford truck purred into view, following the motorcycle out of the gloom. Three short, wiry men leaped from its front seat, slung the three trunks into the enclosed body, slammed doors and jumped back to their seats. Curiously enough, the diplomat had vanished into the dark interior of the truck with those uninspected trunks.

When the first taxicabs started coming out of the *Apgaria's* pier the only sign left on West Street of all this was a single, untended handtruck. That wheelbarrow-like device was to be still there the next morning.

WITHIN THE truck driven by the three yellow-skinned men, the darkness was absolute. But there was sound, queasy sound, and somehow blood-chilling. The scratching of tiny feet, and the shrilling of half-muffled squeals. The rubbing of fabric on fabric, and a low, infinitely evil chuckle.

Wood scraped. A small rectangle of light showed just above

the truck floor. It faded and came again as the vehicle lumbered past street lamps. There was the tang of coffee and the heavier smells of meats, of cheeses. Feet padded softly and key grated in a lock, clicked over.

"Just a minute," a voice said, very low, but diamond hard and cold as steel itself. "You die, Maturo, if you make a move to lift the lid of that trunk!"

"Who… who are you?" the diplomat whispered. "How did you get in here?"

The responding voice, coming out of blackness where the light from that opening did not reach, was emotionless, icy. "Look!"

A click, and faint radiance sprayed over an awesome form, a tall dark threatening shape. It towered seemingly higher than the very ceiling of the truck-body, a torso that was an amorphous fluttering black robe, bat-like; a gray-masked head through whose eye-twin slits menace glinted.

But that which focused Maturo's gaze was neither black body nor gray mask. It was the hand that held the snout of a revolver point-blank at him. A hand ebony-black in its glove—but for the finger curled around the trigger of that gun. That finger was not black but *vividly, awesomely scarlet.*

The Asiatic stared, his lips twitched, a name slid almost soundlessly from between them. *"Red Finger!"*

In Asia, in Europe, even in America itself there were those— governments or individuals—who would reward with untold wealth him who brought proof that Red Finger is no more. Many have tried to win that reward, but the very manner of their death remains to this day unknown. They vanished without trace, into the limbo of darkness.

"Yes!" The steel-hard speech of the master counter-spy replied to the exclamation. "Yes, Maturo. You did not really think that you could liberate those rats inoculated with bubonic plague here in New York's provision district without running up against me? We are not asleep, Maturo. We never sleep."

If the gray hungry rodents once got loose, through the little hole in the truckside and into the warrens here of grain and cheese and vegetables and meat, no earthly power could keep the dread plague from sweeping the country. Of all the schemes Red Finger had checkmated, this was the worst. Women, infants—none will be safe....

And after a month of the plague, that Oriental power could do what she would in a world where there was none but America strong enough to stand in the way of her mad dreams of conquest.

"No!" The Mongol, still motionless, still leaning atop that chest of Black Death, let the monosyllable slide from his lipless mouth. "No. It was too—"

RED FINGER'S eyes glittered with triumph. "Get away from that trunk!" His words dripped into the swaying silence of the moving vehicle. "Get back!"

Maturo paid no attention. "It was too much to hope for," he repeated, "that I might serve my country so much better than I planned... die, Red Finger!" He heaved upright. The trunk-lid came open with his lifting arms and a noisome wave of scuttering, squealing furry gray bodies poured out. Snarling, viperish bearers of the Black Death.

Red Finger's gun flared. Maturo pitched head-first into the chest whence age-old horror was surging—his protective armor forever useless. But the rodents, scenting the food-odors, darted for the opening.

The American hurtled through the dimness. His lank body crashed down, along the truck-wall. The foremost rat squealed wildly as that weight pounded down on it; the counterspy felt the sharp nip of lethal teeth through the folds of his black robe. But that foremost rat could not get out through the hole in the truck-side. For Red Finger's flesh stopped the hole which Maturo has opened for his exit, for the exit of those rodents. Red Finger's flesh—and his soul—writhed in uncontrollable revulsion at the noisome wave of living foulness engulfing him.

Even then, Red Finger's senses were slipping under the sting, the constant, awful sting of the ravenous, angered vermin. The Orientals out front would soon discover what had happened, and release the rats. Even if they did not, *someone* would open the doors....

Red Finger's gun was still in his hand. He lifted it, and furred rodents scuttered away at the movement. He aimed the weapon carefully at the front of the dark truck body, low down. Too low to strike the men on the front seat beyond that unseen partition. Too low to strike anybody but the gasoline tank.

Orange flare sliced the darkness. Again the gun spat. The crash of Red Finger's shots was thunderous in the confined space, and the pungent, choking stench of gasoline filled it. The American's scarlet digit pressed the trigger again.

And the interior of that small truck was an instantaneous holocaust of flame, a blast of blue horror. Then there was no longer any truck at all. There was only a shattered heap of flaming wood and steel in the center of Gansevoort Street. There was only a shambles of charred small bodies of dead rats; of three flaming cadavers. And farther away, blasted to the sidewalk by the force of the explosion, a lank, writhing, flaming figure.

A teamster, inspired, lifted a huge box of damp sawdust in his brawny arms and dumped its contents over Red Finger. It was the one thing that could have saved the American's life— that and the thick wool of his robe, the padded felt of his mask. There was no saw-dust box near enough to save the saffron-skinned men.

LATER, A mummy on a hospital bed, bandaged out of all human semblance, whispered weak words to a startled physician. Yes, there was a serum for the bubonic plague. In New York, enough perhaps for two or three cases, not more.

Enough to send Ford Duane back to his Fourth Street bookshop—months later—scarred, crippled, but ready to go again when the next call comes, as inevitably it must.

DEATH'S RED FINGER

THE SUN was gone below the hot horizon, but its light still lingered, a curious red glow that lay heavily in the long canyon of Fourth Avenue and combined with a strange, breath-bated hush to make the July dusk somehow ominous.

Midway in one crimson-tinged block, Ford Duane stroked the back of a tattered volume with long, sensitive fingers. Tall and gaunt—studiously stooped over the bargain trays outside his dingy bookshop—his ascetic features veiled by their habitual drowsy calm, his eyelids sleepily half-closed, Duane appeared utterly withdrawn from the turmoil of a workaday world, utterly at peace. At peace? *For this man death was a constant, grisly companion, the fear of death was in his every breath!*

From far up the deserted, somnolent street, a raucous call sounded—unintelligible yet filled with an odd, disquieting excitement. Duane half-turned to the cry. To a watcher, if watcher there had been, the movement was indolent, meaningless. But at the corners of his thin nostrils, white spots showed, deepened. Hidden behind his slitted eyelids, tiny lights crawled like minuscule worms.

The lonely figure of a white-shirted newsboy, hurrying toward Duane down the darkening, empty vista, took on a fantastic, unreal aspect. His hoarse call seemed pregnant with dreadful meaning. *"Papers! Final papers!"* The bookseller's skin tightened and a grisly, unacknowledged dread prickled his spine.

The urchin reached him, twisted to him and stood spraddle-legged in front of him.

"Paper? Any these?"

Momentarily, Ford Duane stared uncomprehendingly at the youth who was thrusting a folded sheet fairly into his face. "Post and Telegram. Which one, mister?" Then understanding exploded suddenly in the man's brain. Carelessly, almost mechanically, he took the proffered newspaper and fumblingly paid for it. But behind his drowsy mask, his every nerve—every brain cell—was suddenly quiveringly alive.

"Final papers. Joinal! Telegram!" The youngster's shouts faded into the lamplit darkness. Duane stuffed his purchase into a sagging side-pocket of his gray alpaca coat, started on the nightly routine of dragging the bargain boxes within the pamphlet-hung door of his store. *"Paper."* The boy had said. *"Any these?"* And then, *"Post and Telegram."* It was no accident that the phrases had been so oddly twisted, no accident *that the initial letters of the first three words had been identical.* P! A! T!

P. A. T. In many and various forms, those three letters had come to Duane; in a huckster's shout, in an old man's quavering offer of an ancient folio, in a beggar's plea. Each time, inevitably, men had died in the night. Now again, the mysterious signal had come, and muscles bunched along the gaunt jaw of the dealer in dusty antique books, and in very blue eyes veiled by drowsy lids an eager light glowed.

Ford Duane locked the store door from within, wheeled

to face the dim, mysterious gloom of the crowded bookstacks inside. His gaze warily probed the black pools of shadow between them, through which he slowly waded. He was like a taut wire, vibrant for any hint of danger. Even here, even in his own small store—*above all in his own store*—he must be infinitely on the alert.

At the rear of the shop, grime-encrusted curtains rustled, parted and swung shut. Duane's hand found a familiar switch. It clicked and yellow light spilled from a pendant bulb to edge with harshness a touseled iron cot, a bare wooden table, a rickety chair. A steel shutter was tightly clamped over the single window, held there by a bar queerly too new, too thick for the stock of old books it ostensibly guarded....

DUANE JERKED the newly-bought newspaper from his pocket, spread it on the table. Standing, he thumbed through page after page of the voluminous sheet. His feverish glance scanned each broadside, rejected it. Then, suddenly, breath hissed sharply from between his clenched teeth and the furious search was at an end.

It was an advertisement at which the bookseller stared! Crudely drawn, a tailor squatted crosslegged on a ship's bridge and sewed a patch on a limp pair of trousers. And beneath was the caption, black against wiggly waves on which the pictured craft rode:

*P*INCUS; *A*BLE *T*AILOR

Once more the fateful initials P-A-T! Once more! But below them was a hodge-podge of selling talk, a conglomerate of forced alliteration and mixed metaphor. What meaning could there be in this claptrap for Duane?

Yes. Able Tailor, not Able Seaman. If you want to safely sail the suspicious seas of style, men, whatever your nationality or politics you will not resort to artisans whose skill is unknown but will select the famous Abe Pincus captain of your sartorial ship. Wherever well-dressed men are observed, there his navy blue serge suits are seen, made from material guaranteed all wool and a yard wide. Investigate his values....

Duane's examination of the advertisement was brief. He

shoved the paper aside, clearing the top of the table. White-scrubbed, the expanse of pine-wood was exactly the same as that of a thousand other cheap kitchen tables worn by long use. Exactly? Some manipulation of the man's fingers at the edge of that top, too fast to be clearly seen, and a thin, rectangular panel of wood lifted at the very center, as if pushed from beneath. Ford pried at it with quivering finger-nails, it hinged upward like a lid, and a shallow recess was revealed beneath.

The man bent over the table, staring into that secret pocket. There was only one thing in the depression, something outré as the mode of concealment itself. Extricated, it was revealed as a flat piece of gray paper, thick and stiff. It might almost have been half of a shirtboard, except that it was pierced by a number of rectangular holes, each an eighth of an inch wide and about a half-inch long. These perforations, though parallel, were placed apparently at random—made no appreciable pattern.

Duane slapped down the lid of the hiding place and it sank level with the rest of the tabletop. The line of separation was altogether invisible. The next instant, the place where the mysterious receptacle had been was once more covered by the news sheet, the ad that so poinantly intrigued Duane's attention uppermost.

The bookseller picked up the perforated cardboard, laid it over that advertisement. Some lines in the illustration seemed to match faint traces, on the gray stencil and these Ford matched up meticulously. Words stared through the holes. The man's lips tightened to a straight, grim line as he read:

—suspicious—men—nationality—unknown—

observed—navy—yard—Investigate—

"All right, mister!" A suave voice was velvety behind Duane. *"You're covered!"*

The bookseller froze. Only his hands were alive, tightening on the table-edge.

For an infinite moment in the little chamber there was an appalled silence as panic and despair gripped Duane's soul. They had tracked him down at last—his implacable enemies. His sanctuary was violated, his masquerade discovered. The long game was at an end, finally—irretrievably at its inevitable end!

"Good evening!" Duane's voice was low-pitched, steady. But he stared straight ahead of him as he spoke. His slightest movement, he knew, would bring a bullet crashing into his spine and these last few instants of life were somehow too sweet to lose.

"Keep your hands way out from your sides and turn around. Slowly." There was excitement in the intruder's tones and gloating triumph. Half the Chancelleries of Europe had laid a price upon the head of Ford Duane. The American ace in the underground war that eternally is waged between spy and counterspy, *saboteur* and secret agent—his slayer would gain at one stroke honor, and wealth. *"Turn around, I say!"*

HIS ARMS angling out stiffly, Duane obeyed. At one side of the cubicle he called home, the narrow wall had apparently slid aside to disclose a dark, shelf-lined niche beyond. Within this crouched a weazened, bent creature. In a taloned, grimy hand, a blue-barreled automatic snouted at Ford. Beady eyes peered at him from beneath a shock of unkempt, shaggy black hair. The fellow's shabby clothing was dust-smeared; there was a streak of soot across one sunken cheek. Something of a rat's vileness clung to him, and all a rat's cruel savagery.

Duane's mouth twitched wryly. "Feodor Dvatich," he exclaimed, softly. His last hope was gone that this might be an ordinary stickup—and with it the last need for pretence. "Evidently I was too trusting the night I recovered the chart of the M-6 mobilization plan from you and trusted your promise to leave America forever."

Dvatich's lips curled back from yellow, pointed teeth in an evil leer. "Fifty thousand dollars a certain power would have paid me for those plans. You robbed me of that. But now your death will give me many times that, hein?"

"Perhaps."

"Of a certainty. Feodor Dvatich would otherwise have not wasted his time spying on other spies for the sole purpose of watching for you to appear so that he might track you down."

Reluctant admiration sounded in Duane's tones. "So that is how...."

"That is how I discovered your lair and the secret entrance to it." Yellow teeth showed again in a vainglorious smile. "Yes. That is how I succeeded where others have failed." He broke off, the muzzle of his pistol jutted toward the American. "But enough. If you believe in prayer, pray now, mister, because I fire when I count three. One—!"

Incredible how swift thought can be when only seconds remain in which to think! There was nothing to regret. In his few short years, Duane had packed excitement enough for a centenarian, had had innumerable narrow escapes. His luck had run out, that was all.

"Two—!"

He would like just once to have had his country know what it was he had done for it—just once to have been praised publicly, publicly rewarded. This working in the dark, receiving disguised messages—Good Lord! There was one on his table now! If he kicked out now, it might be days before the little gray man in Washington knew it. Meantime….

Half the Atlantic fleet was in the Navy Yard basin! Were they in danger! Danger he was being sent to avert?

"Thr—!" Duane's long leg lashed out, a released spring, caught a rung of the cane-bottomed chair, flung it in an explosive arc to crash against Dvatich's chest. Gun-bark blazed orange flame, something zizzed past the tall man's cheek, and he had flung himself after that chair. His flailing fist splashed a yellow-toothed face into bloody pulp. The smoking automatic blazed once more, once only. Agony squealed in that hidden room—the sound was hardly human. The sudden flurry of action was over. A broken, unmoving body lay crumpled on the bloodstained floor.

Ford Duane's eyes were hard, expressionless as agate, his face carved marble as he came erect, lifting the limp corpse of the would-be assassin and throwing it over one shoulder. The drowsy dealer in second-hand books was completely obliterated, replaced by a grim-featured, tight-jawed robot who stalked into the niche whence the killer had appeared. With his free hand, Duane tugged at one of the shelves within, it moved toward him, the wall to which it was attached came with it. Behind, wooden stairs, slick with greasy damp, dipped down into darkness. The tall man and his grisly burden went slowly down into that darkness.

A HALF-HOUR later, Ford Duane was once more stooped over the gray cardboard stencil, once more reading the words outlined. There was no sign of what had so recently occurred in this back-room space—no stain on the linoleum-covered floor. No change, except that a picture had been moved—was it to conceal a bullet-hole?

To one side of the advertisement that Duane studied, inconspicuous headlines topped a shipnews item buried inconspicuously on an inside page of the newspaper:

ALL EUROPE AN ARMED ENCAMPMENT—
PROPAGANDA HERE WORSE THAN 1914!
Returning Ambassador Says Only American
Neutrality Prevents War!

A SINGLE light burned high up in the archway of the Brooklyn Navy Yard's Sand Street gate. Within the sharp-cut cone of its glare a stalwart marine stood stiffly erect, rifle aslant across a shoulder brightly blue. Lithe, young and strong in body he was, this soldier of the sea, but the outlines of his broad-planed features were somehow blurred where they should have been sharp and clean. Paint pouches showed under his troubled eyes and a faint hint of looseness touched—just touched—his thick-lipped mouth.

Darkness invested the sleazy dwellings facing the yard's high wall; a darkness and a silence that were yet somehow creepily, foully alive. The marine's glance slid across to them. It singled out one drab tenement, and his lips twisted with bitterness and distaste.

His hand tightened on his rifle's butt. The shadows in the unlit vestibule of that draggled house had suddenly seemed to move. They were moving! The darkness there split; an inky blot detached itself, was gliding across the cobbles. It disappeared in the deeper blackness of the nearer wall, but a hiss of sound told of movement there. The scrape of fabric sliding against brick came nearer, stopped.

"Johnee!" The voice from just beyond the gateway lamp's illumination was low-pitched, guarded, but there was a lilting feminine sweetness in it that willy-nilly thrilled in the young soldier's veins. "Johnee! Come here!"

The marine was a motionless, graven image, save that in his right temple, a pulse thumped, thumped. "Johnee!" the voice came again, demanding—and seductive. "Just one leetle meen-ute!"

There was promise in the dulcet accents, promise, and obscurely, threat.

Private John Boles seemed to fight a force from outside himself, to fight unavailingly. His feet shuffled as it turned him toward the summons, as it jerked him out of the glare into blinding lightlessness.

"Johnee, heart of my heart!" A warm body was close against him, warm lips were reaching for his. Redolence of woman's hair, of a woman infinitely desirable, was dizzyingly in his nostrils. His free arm was tight around a soft, palpitant form....

And swung it, almost roughly then, away from him. "Lola! Damn it! I told yuh to stay away from here! Want to get me court-martialed?

The girl squirmed in his hold, sobbed. "Oh Johnee! You deed not theenk of courtmartials biffore, whan you tell me you luf me. Deed you lie?"

"No!" The word was a groan, wrested from his light throat. "I didn't lie. I was nuts about yuh…."

"Then whyee…?"

"Till yuh propositioned me las' night to let some guy slip through the gate. I shoulda turned yuh in, Lola."

"But Johnee! Eet was the money I was theenking of, the money he would pay. Just theenk, you could buy your deescharge an' we could be married. Wance more I beg you…."

"Yuh—!"

Still low-pitched, almost inaudible, still the marine's expletive rammed Lola's whispered words down her throat. "If you pull that once more, I'll—"

Thud! The impact of the sandbag against the back of Private John Boles' skull was almost soundless. He crumpled, like a ripped flour sack, and as he slid slowly to the unseen ground, a hand came over his shoulder to grasp his rifle so that it would not clatter an alarm on the concrete.

"Oh, you've keeled…!"

"Shut up, fool, or you'll give the show away!" This new voice was gruff, even in undertone, and vibrant with urgency. "Help me with his clothes, quick. We have only five minutes till his relief is due!"

FIVE MINUTES later, to the dot, the huge portal opened for the Sergeant of the Guard and the marine who was to take Private Boles' place. The waiting sentry was not quite in his proper position, so that the shadows of the gate's embrasure fell across his features. But he presented arms punctiliously, about-faced smartly at the Sergeant's "Dismiss!" and strode off into the yard's obscurity.

The Sergeant yawned sleepily. This guard-post business was just red-tape in peace time, he thought. Just an excuse to keep a man up nights.

Huge cranes, mountainous derricks, were interlaced against a leaden, overcast sky. Between towering workshop structures impenetrable darkness weltered, hiding the now stealthy progress of the man who wore John Boles' uniform. The marine barracks were far behind him now. What business could he have in this portion of the yard? What business had those others here, for that matter, those two furtive figures that suddenly joined him, as though spawned by the tar-barrel murk? A low chuckle sounded from one of the skulking trio.

"That was too easy. If you had had a half-hour more, you could have let an army in and no one the wiser for it."

"We are enough," the low-voiced reply came. "That which you carry makes us more powerful than any army."

The row of tall buildings between which they had been hurrying fell away. A dim nimbus of light encompassed them. The gray glow of the city reflected from the overarching cloud dome. They were in an open space....

"Careful," the apparent leader said sharply. "Watch your feet."

That halted the prowlers—on the edge of what seemed a cliff dropping down and down in terraced descent. Far below there was a tiny glint of water. Vision cleared, and it became evident that they were standing on the brink of a gigantic, man-built basin. Ahead, a vast gray bulk loomed, like some unbelievably enormous prehistoric monster asleep in the depression.

"The *Missitucky* gentlemen!" the putative marine announced. "Pride of the American navy!" There was something obscene in the way he lipped the words, something suggestive of a gourmet about to devour a Lucullan feast. A murmur came from his companions, the smacking of lips that drooled lewd anticipation.

A chaos of long timbers jutted out from the sides of the drydock, holding the dreadnaught erect in its ways. From a few paces to the left, a spiderly gangplank soared out over vacancy to reach the battleship's deck. Somehow in the drab dimness over there, the measured thump of pacing feet sounded. The shadowy figure of a lonely deck watch appeared from around a turret, pounded slowly aft.

"All right, G-X, take him." The leader's snapped command was scarcely audible, but one of the others dropped to his knees. His arms lifted. He was aiming a squat, grotesquely thick gun. The sound it made was only the dull *ffft* of an air rifle, but aboard the *Missitucky,* the solitary sailor pitched forward, pudded down, asprawl.

"Quick! Before anyone sees him!" Three silhouettes flitted across the gangplank stark against a leaden sky. They clotted momentarily about that pathetic blotch on the vessel's deck.

Then they were out of sight from the dockside and nothing broke the wide, faintly luminous expanse of steel....

For minutes there was no sign of a living presence there. Then, once more the measured thump of pacing feet sounded and from behind the forward turret, the dim-described figure of a sailor appeared to pound slowly aft in the appointed round of the dreadnaught's deck watch....

DOWN THROUGH the silent, deserted hold of the battleship, two stealthy skulkers descended, their steps almost inaudible on the steel companionways. He who was garbed as a marine led the way, his whole frame vibrant as a poisonous bushmaster snake tracking its prey. The other, more timorous in his progress, was shapeless in the voluminous topcoat he wore despite the heat. He was carrying something, a large box—carrying it gingerly as though he were in a deathly fear of it.

"Here we are!" the fake marine breathed. In the dim reaches of the lowermost hold, illuminated by a single pendant light, the vast loom of the vessel's engine-room stretched away. "Get busy!"

The other man lurched past him, deposited his mysterious burden close against the base of a gigantic Diesel engine, did something with shaking hands. A sharp metallic click splintered the silence, was repeated, became a ticking.

"All set, H-T?" he asked. "You're sure?"

His vis-à-vis turned. "Sure. In twenty minutes there will be no more *Missitucky.*"

"And the explosion that destroys it will set the world aflame. Look here!" He held out the strange metallic fragment. "When they find this in the wreckage, they will be sure they know which nation inspired the deed." With the muzzle of his revolver he pointed out words stamped into the metal: "Creusot Frères et Cie."

The other chuckled. "I'll say they will be! What price 'no entangling alliances' then?"

"A hundred for a pfennig!" The supposed marine bent swiftly to place that lying piece of evidence on the floor. "These aloof Americans will be begging us to ally ourselves with them, and we will—on our own terms. But we'd better get out of here in a hurry. Come!" He turned to the hatchway behind him....

And he did not take the pace he had intended! A tall, unearthly figure was advancing out of its darkness, as though spawned by deathly night.

But that which froze the *saboteurs* into fear-struck rigidity was the one, black-gloved hand that was visible, clutching a wide barreled, queer weapon. Not the weapon itself. These prowlers of the dark were, after all, brave men. But it was the finger that curled about the trigger, the *scarlet* finger that told them who it was that had tracked them down. The dread name dripped from the spy leader's white lips:

"Red Finger! Gott in Himmel! Es ist der Roter Finger!"

Yes, they were brave men. No cowards take part in the secret war. But to see before them the avatar of their trade—to be caught in *flagrante delicto* by HIM was enough to break nerves of the stoutest villain, enough to make the hottest blood turn to water in gelid veins.

"Red Finger!" The planter of the infernal machine whispered it. "God have mercy!"

DEATH'S RED FINGER

THEN SILENCE, through which cut the tick, tick, tick of the bomb. Silence for a long, accusing minute, while Red Finger stood statuesque, ominous, and the destroyers cringed spineless before him. Silence, till a husky, intonationless voice dripped from behind the gray mask:

"Yes, Adolf Mauerer. Red Finger. You did not really hope to escape me, did you?"

The American's strange gun was rock-steady, jutting point-blank at the others. "Shut off that machine, Mauerer. Shut it off." His command thudded, word by slow word, into an atmosphere somehow unnaturally thick.

H-T started to move, but somehow Mauerer's shoulder was in his way, halting him. "Impossible, Red Finger," the latter responded, in a dead, flat voice. *"Once started, the bomb cannot again be stopped!"*

Tick. Tick. Tick. It was as if Death's heels clicked, approaching slowly, inexorably. Tick. Tick. Tick.

"No?" There was no emotion in the masked man's tones. "Then we stay here, we three, till it explodes."

Tick. Tick. Tick.

Mauerer was immovable, indomitable as the implacable enemy who faced him. Tickticktick. But his companion's frame was taken by an ague, by a shiver, imperceptible at first, that grew more and more violent, until....

"No," a wild, thin shriek rang out. "No! I will not die! Ach Gott! I will not die *like dot!"* He twisted, Mauerer struck at him viciously. The blow staggered him, he plunged to the floor. A soft hiss sounded from Red Finger's gun, a jet of fine mist spat from

81

it, sprayed Mauerer's face. The spy-leader lurched away, clawing at his throat. Crumpled. H-T was crawling across the deck, writhing toward the mechanism that ticked Death's approach. He reached it, scrabbled at it....

Red Finger whirled to the pound of a footfall on a steel companionway. A sailor was coming down the stairs, a sailor from beneath whose canted cap blonde lair strayed. The American's tension relaxed, he started to turn away.

"Fritz," the man at the infernal machine squealed. "Get him! Kill him!"

A knife flashed into the sailor's hand and he launched from the stairs in a wild leap at Red Finger, the lethal steel arcking. Red Finger's gun spat mist again.

The sailor stumbled, slid lifelessly to lie in a crumpled heap over the body of his leader. Red Finger jerked around to the last of the trio. "Shut it off!" he barked. "Or we'll all go up."

The man's shaking hand tugged at the apparatus. "It's stuck," he whimpered. "I cannot push the lever over!"

He popped to his feet, his mouth aslaver, his eyes utterly insane. "Let me out," he squealed. "Let me out!" He hurtled toward the hatchway, his face twisted to a semblance of ratlike ferocity, hurtled past Red Finger. The American let him go, dropped to his knees before the ticking bomb. There were seconds left, perhaps he could yet get it stopped. He had seen what the other had been trying to do....

The retreating footsteps of the man whom fear had driven mad resounded loudly up the steel stairway, but it did not drown out the awful tickticktick of the infernal machine. Red Finger tore at the switches, ripped his gloves. His fingers dripped blood. Tickticktick....

"Halt!" A sharp challenge, distance-muffled, rang out. The counterspy was conscious of the pound of many feet, far above. Good Lord! There were men on board now, they were coming down here, they would be caught in the explosion. He had to—get this damn' thing—stopped.

"Ah!" Suddenly it was done. The obdurate lever slid over, the ticking was stilled. A warrant-officer pounded into the engine room, revolver in hand. Red Finger rose to meet him, hands above his head. "Keep those others out," he snapped, "till I have a chance to talk with you."

THE MORNING sun burned down into the canyon that is Fourth Avenue. Ford Duane sat in a broken-backed swivel chair in the doorway of his second-hand bookshop, and yawned. Then he continued his languid perusal of the morning newspaper. One item seemed to arrest his attention momentarily.

"Early this morning," it said, "the harbor police found the bodies of three men floating in the Bay. The bodies were clothed only in underwear. There were no marks of violence or any other indication of how they had died or who they were."

Duane yawned again. It was lucky that the commandant of the Navy Yard had listened to reason. A trial, even a military trial, would inevitably have involved the name of Mauerer's nation. Skilled propagandists would have ferreted out the truth, published it....

It was peaceful here in the hot sun....

RED FINGER
MEETS HIS MATCH

EXCITEMENT RAN like a fever through the manifold arteries of New York. Broadway quivered with its tremor, manifest in the fluttering of starry flags which tossed above a honking, eager rush of traffic and made vivid the drab, towering walls of the world's most famous street. It surged tumultuous through the side-streets. Its hot thrill shuddered along Fifth Avenue and the broad sidewalks of the jeweled thoroughfare became murmurous and black with the thousands gathering to wait for the Procession that not yet for hours would file between the Golden Lamps. It hammered in the subways, buzzed in the 'El' trains, the buses, the street-cars whose racketing rush brought more and ever more of the city's myriads to the city's heart.

The pulse of that heart was a vast throb in the air, a measured tuneless rhythm of drums beating martial time. Drums everywhere! The whole vast metropolis was their sounding board. Into every nook and cranny of the sprawling town their dull beat, beat, beat penetrated—into every alley, and every street....

Even into the musty drowse of the Fourth Avenue block which is known as the Port of Ancient Books came that pervading throb, even into the dim dusk within the sleepiest of the sleepy, second-hand bookshops there—that of Ford Duane. Beat, beat, beat, it stirred even the dead dust filming the lofty, crowded shelves of forgotten tomes. Only Duane himself seemed immune to it, the young-old man whose drooped, tired-seeming lids veiled eyes somehow too blue, too keen for the lethargy of his tall, bent figure—for the dull, uneventful round of life in this black-eddy of the city's torrential stream.

Too keen? Perhaps they were not keen enough, those eyes. Perhaps some time they would not be quite watchful enough to forestall the sudden, flashing flicker of death which at any moment might strike at their owner. For death, to Ford Duane, was an ever-present, ever-imminent threat. There was a price on his head in half the chancelleries of the Eastern Hemisphere. There were those whose lust to slash steel into his heart—to blast lead into his flesh—needed no price to whet it. Sooner or later he knew, one of those must discover who the shambling bookseller he pretended to be really was. And then....

From somewhere far off, a filament of silver sound threaded the beat, beat of the drums, a bugle singing the *ta-tit, ta-tit, ta-lit taaa* of 'Assembly.'

"Queer, isn't it, that they couldn't find anything but war music to play today?" There was a strangely sweet huskiness in the voice of the girl who turned to Duane from the shelf where she had been browsing. "You would think that He would hate the bugles and the drums and the brass bands to whose blare the soldiers have always marched to slaughter as much as He hates war itself."

Dark-suited and dark-hatted though her slender, supple small figure was, she glowed, somehow, in the grimy twilight of the grimy shop. It must be some transparency of her skin, the book-

85

man thought, that gave that effect of an inner light, or maybe it was the way tawny lights glinted in her russet hair.

"Even He has to use the old, primitive ways to put His idea across," he responded. Both were capitalizing the masculine pronoun, neither seemed to doubt that the other understood who was meant. In New York that day it *could* mean only one man. "Always in the past parades have meant war. This one means peace—but it's a parade anyway."

"YES! A parade to tell Europe and Asia and Africa their propaganda has failed." Her gray eyes were shining now with an almost fanatical luminescence. "To tell them America will never again take part in their quarrels—that America is a land

86

of peace. Thousands—hundreds of thousands—following Him through the streets, tramping after Him with all the fervor of a Crusade. Shouting, and meaning their shouts, "No more war! No more war!"

The girl's speech was exalted, but then, the speech of most men these days was exalted, led to the heights as they were by the vision and the strength of the Great Man whose triumph the Peace Procession signalized.

"Never in all the world," the girl went on, "has there been such a march of victory as this one. Of His victory after all these months of lonely fighting, and struggle, and almost of despair. Victory over the Old World's wily tricks to bring us in on one side or the other, knowing they must have us or be defeated. Victory over the shouters here at home, the jingoes, the profiteers, the honest but misguided zealots who still believe the way to Peace must be mired by the tears and the blood of war. A glorious parade!"

"Glorious." Ford Duane repeated the word, but no exaltation showed in his face that was too seamed, too grim for his youth. *"And dangerous!"*

"Dangerous!" She gasped, her long, flexible fingers coming up to her breast. "What—what do you mean?" The drum-pulse was suddenly ominous in the hush of the bookstore, suddenly a dull and boding threat. For a long minute, a throbbing silence lasted, while Duane covertly studied her, and then he spoke.

"The city is like a tinder box," he explained slowly, wondering what there was about this girl that made him speak—he whose very existence so long had depended on silence. "The city and the whole country. Like a powder magazine needing only a spark to set off an explosion that will blast the world apart. The very frenzy for peace to which He has lashed us might, in the merest instant, be transformed to just as virulent, just as overpowering a tornado of destruction. And," Duane's voice dropped very low, "someone might be planning, right now, to do exactly that."

"How?" she gasped, her lips suddenly white. "How could anyone…?"

"Suppose—suppose that four hours from now, while He is riding at the head of His Procession, He were to be shot down? What would happen, do you think…?"

"They would tear his assassin into little pieces!" Her hands made small rending motions, somehow horrible. "Into such little pieces he might never have lived at all."

THE FURY that shook her was a strange and deadly passion in so slight a frame, but Duane went on, evenly. "And suppose it were discovered that the killer was not a madman but an emissary of one of the nations who are at each other's throats across the sea?"

"We'd sweep them off the face of the earth!" the girl flared. "Every man, every woman in America would rush to arms and…" she caught herself. Her eyes widened, their pupils dilating till they were staring, black pits. "Oh!" she moaned. "I see—but that would be insane. It would be mass suicide…!"

Duane's countenance was a gray, bleak mask, his mouth a straight, grim line somehow tortured. "Neither insane nor suicide. *If the wrong nation were blamed for the deed!*"

"No," the russet-haired girl groaned. "No. Men are not so horrible. Not so vile…."

"Dulce et decorum est," Duane shrugged, *"pro patria mori.* Sweet and proper is it to die for one's country. Not only to die. To make of oneself an abomination in the memory of decent men." All the repression of his lonely calling, all his loathing of the human vermin he fought in the slimy, underground spy-world of the Endless War, spewed bitterness into his unaccustomed speech. "Not long ago the venerable Chancellor of a nation then the leader of the world's culture forged a telegram to plunge half a continent into war, and boasted of it in his memoirs. Why I…."

He stopped, startled, dismayed at his own garrulity. He had almost betrayed himself to this snip of a maid with a tiny, pert face and haunting eyes. What was there about her that shook him so out of the icy, impersonal calm to which necessity had schooled him? What…? The tramp, tramp of marching feet slogged in. A detachment of men were passing, marching soldier-like in straight lines, in perfect step to the thump, thump, thump of the omnipresent drumbeat. Marching soldier-like— but not in uniform, bearing no rifles. Wearing instead, proudly as an accolade of knighthood, each a broad, white satin ribbon across his breast with the single, scarlet word blazoned upon it: PEACE!

"Oh!" the girl exclaimed. "I must be going. I've got to join my unit." She started for the door.

"Wait!" The word seemed torn from Ford Duane without any volition of his own. "Wait! I can't let you go without knowing whether I'll ever see you again, without knowing who you are."

She turned at the doorway. A mysterious smile hovered faintly about her pale lips, a brooding compassion tinctured her eyes with mystery. "We may not be permitted to meet again," she half-whispered in that husky, heart-tearing voice of hers. "But I was instructed to tell you that my name is Patricia Ann Towndell." Then she was gone, vanishing somehow into the pulsing, excited vastness of out-doors as though she had been only a glamorous dream.

DUANE MADE no move to follow her. "Patricia-Ann-Towndell," he repeated, low-toned. "She's one of us!" There was no joy in his voice. There was only a great fear for her. For to be 'one of us' meant to know no slightest moment of safety, meant to walk always in the Valley of the Shadow of Death. And she—so fragile—so utterly glamorous....

But he was wasting time—they both had wasted time they had no right to waste. *Patricia Ann Towndell!* P—A—T. Three letters out of all the alphabet, but three letters with a grisly meaning. In a huckster's shout, in a beggar's plea, a newsboy's hawking cry, they had come before this to Ford Duane to herald a message from a closely guarded little room in Washington. And each time, secret forces had moved in a gray and secret underworld and someone had mysteriously died.

But where was the message now?

Duane's blue eyes darted about his tiny shop, saw nothing that was not there before she came—yes! On the floor where she had stood for a little while glowing with her inner light, a filmy scarf lay. Only a pastel-hued length of gossamer georgette....

Duane bent to it and as he picked it up his long, sensitive fingers were trembling slightly, almost imperceptibly.

He straightened, moved slowly between the ceiling-high stacks of his stock-in-trade toward the curtain hung from a sagging pole that screened off the rear. He moved slowly, lethargically, but every nerve of his gaunt body was taut, every sense tense with vigilance. A little muscle twitched in his cheek....

Ford Duane reached the narrow back room where a rumpled cot, a rickety chair and a knife-hacked table furnished drab living quarters for what the world knew as his drab life. He left the curtain open, so that he might have a clear view of anyone coming into the shop—so that anyone coming in might have a clear view of him—slumped on the chair and apparently lost in his habitual brown study. But, peculiarly enough, the curtain-edge just hid the table-top from such a possible customer, and on that table-top the flimsy scarf was spread flat.

Apparently half-asleep, Duane's gaze slid searchingly along the cobwebby fabric's hem, along the tiny stitches which fashioned that hem. Those meticulous, hand-sewn stitches were not quite of even length, as hand-sewn stitches can never be. Some were almost infinitesimally longer than others. Long and short, short and long, they made a pattern. Dash-dot, dot-dash.... They made letters, not in the Continental Morse Code of wireless communication which might be read by anyone guessing their secret, but in another, similar code whose key lay only in Duane's brain, and in the brain of the gray little man who hid in that barred Capitol chamber and directed the invisible army in whose ranks Ford Duane was a single cog.

Dash-dot, dot-dash.... The message was read at least. Duane sighed, rose, stretching his awkward, gawky length. Behind their veiling lids tiny, lurid lights crawled in his eyes.

THE CROWD was growing restive now, along Fifth Avenue. The crowd! It wasn't a crowd any longer. It was a gargantuan, many-celled entity, packing the long street from building line to building line, from Washington Arch to the circle of filling stations and movie houses at Central Park's northern end. It was a single soul, the soul of an America reborn, welded into unity by the flaming words of Him whom they awaited, merged into one by the beat, beat of the drums, by the throbbing, brazen rhythm of the bands about which those who were to march were forming.

They were playing a single tune, those bands, and by some miracle of a common inspiration they were playing it in perfect unison. The throbbing beat of it pulsed in the brains of the millions, pulsed in their throats, broke forth in a vast Niagara of sound, a song such as never before the world had heard, a song sung by a city.

The thunder of it surged from the streets, surged upward to the sky. The thunder and the glory of that marching hymn:

> Never more as soldiers march we on to war,
> Murder, loot and rapine know we never more.
> Peace and love for all men, calling no one foe,
> Beastlike into battle never shall we go....

And the swelling surf of the chorus:

Hear us, God, we pledge thee,
War we wage no more!

They broke into great, pealing shouts, "No more war! *No more war!* NO MORE WAR!" that seemed to fill the high dome of the sky, to roll on and on over the tossing sea where great, gray steel monsters prowled seeking one another to belch flame and destruction, to reach the old, disillusioned lands across whose ancient soil the mailed feet of Mars still strode.

The song and the shouts roared against the flag-bedizened facades of the tall buildings along the Avenue, beat into them. Beat into the four structures fronting Rockefeller Center, over each of whose portals the name of a different alien nation is graven. Beat into a large showroom in one of them, a suavely carpeted room behind whose plate-glass window three smirking wax dummies displayed the glittering best that far-off nation offered for sale to America.

"They're due to change that tune very soon," a man in that room said softly. "Sooner than they think." His English was perfect—too perfect—its very precision betraying that it was not his mother-tongue. He leaned against a crystal-fronted show-case, frock-coated, swarthy, a faint sneer lifting the corners of his thin, cruel lips, his glittering, black eyes somehow vulturine....

A STOCKIER, not quite so dapper individual turned from gazing out of the window at that incredible crowd and stroked his trim vandyke with fingers the color of a dead fish's belly. "Maybe, Garon. Maybe." He shrugged. "But I...."

"But what?" Garon queried, his countenance darkening.

"What troubles you, Fator, my friend? You yourself admit that our plans are faultless."

The other shrugged. "Faultless, yes. But I have seen faultless plans fail before, because of one man. Because of...."

"The one they call Red Finger? The American counter-spy who almost singed your feathers, last year?" Garon's smile was a taunting, evil thing. "I don't think he'll bother us. I have made certain arrangements...."

"Arrangements!" Fator exclaimed, "What arrangements?"

Garon seemed quite pleased with himself. "Simple ones, Fator. Simply to dispose of this redoubtable Red Finger before he disposes of us."

"But—but no one knows who he is or where he exists between his exploits. He vanishes...."

"Bosh! He has to be somewhere, and he has to receive orders from someone. Long ago I made it my business to discover who that someone is—long before our present project was even dreamed of. When we did start work, I let that someone learn of our little enterprise, with the proper inflection, of course. I had his messenger spotted, and...."

"And intercepted the message!"

"No, fool! That would have been what you would have done. Red Finger would have been warned by some other channel, and—*poof!* No. My men had orders to follow that messenger and.... But you shall hear for yourself what occurred."

The whine of the freight elevator, far to the rear, had interrupted him. The two turned to the bronze doors, waited in a silence emphasized rather than broken by the terrific roar outside. The doors opened....

The fellow who emerged was dressed as a porter, and his broad, powerful frame stamped him as a very capable one. He stood at the elevator gate, twisting his cap in his hand.

"Well," Garon burst out, with the excitability of his race. "Report, Sloman. Successful, of course?"

The fellow shook his head, and there was fear in his eyes. "We were on her heels every minute, heard every word she spoke to anyone. There was nothing suspicious, she gave no paper to anyone, mailed no letter, 'phoned no one. It's a dud...."

The *saboteur* was livid with rage. "Ass!" he squealed. "Imbecile. She fooled you. She must have fooled you. And you let her give you the slip...."

"No, chief," Sloman interrupted. "We did not."

"What do you mean?"

"The time was growing short and nothing had developed, so we decided to bring her here."

"Here!" Garon and Fator exclaimed simultaneously. "Here!"

"Yes, Chief." Sloman turned and went back into the elevator. Almost at once he was out again, bent under the weight of a trunk on his shoulders such as valuable frocks are shipped in. He let it slide, unlocked it and threw open its lid.

THE TWO others were leaning over the trunk's side almost before it was opened. "But she is beautiful," popped from Fator's lips. "A flower...!"

"A flower of evil to us if we can't make her talk—and quickly!" Between them, Garon and Sloman had the girl out of the trunk.

95

She was gagged, bound hand and foot, but the gray eyes under her rumpled, russet hair were defiant. Garon jerked at the gag, jerked it free.

"Who is he?" he splurted, wasting no time. "Who is the one to whom you took the message?"

The girl's mouth worked. Then: "This is an outrage! To be drugged in a taxi in the heart of New York, to wake up tied up and boxed like a piece of merchandise. I'll report...."

"You'll report nothing, and you'll tell us what we want to know, or else...." The fact that Garon did not complete his threat was somehow more ominous than if he had. The girl paled, made a decision.

"I won't bluff, then. That's no use. But I'm not bluffing when I tell you that you won't get anything out of me. Not if you kill me."

"No?" Garon purred. "No?" He was feline, cruelly feline. "We shall not kill you, yet. But you shall speak, my dear. You shall speak... Fator," he turned to his aide, his voice crackling. "In that drawer back there are scissors and an alcohol lamp. We shall see whether or not the little lady will tell us what we want to know."

The shorter man found the articles called for, came back with them. The girl flinched at the snap of the match that lit the lamp, watched with dilated pupils the points of the scissors grow red, then white in the flame. At last Garon turned back to her, and his eyes were black, demoniac pits in a Satanic face.

"For the last time," he purred, "who is Red Finger?"

Her throat throbbed, and the arteries at the sides of her neck fluttered with her terror. But her gaze, fixed on the white-hot metal points, was defiant and her lips tight-shut. Garon lowered the thing he held, lowered it till the smell of the hot metal was in her nostrils, till she had to close her lids against the glare.

"That won't help you," he whispered. "Flesh burns through, and eyes can be blinded. Will you tell us who Red Finger is?"

"No!" the girl gasped, and felt the gag go back into her mouth. That was, she knew, to stopper her scream, which might be heard above the thunder of the crowd. Heat from those terrible scissors seared her lids, she smelled the acrid tang of singed lashes....

And suddenly the heat was gone as someone pounded on the outer door. "Just a minute," Garon called out. "Into the trunk!" he hissed. "Quick. Into the trunk with her!"

SHE WAS back in the trunk, the straps that had held her rigid before buckled about her again, the lid closed down.

"Hear us, God, we pledge thee," roared in as Garon opened the door to his unlooked for callers. *"War we wage no more!"* Three men in the uniform of the city police stood out there.

"What is it, gentlemen?" the alien asked, courteously. "What can I do for you?"

"Sorry, mister," one of the policemen said. "You'll have to get out of here. Federal orders are to clear all buildings along the parade route, for fear of something happening."

"But this is a semi-diplomatic establishment," Garon objected. "Surely those orders cannot apply to us. We're representatives of a friendly country."

"Sure. Sure you are. That's why you ought to be anxious to get out. Suppose He was killed by a bullet from some window along here and we couldn't make out just where? It would be just too bad if you were found in here, wouldn't it?"

"Good Lord! There is no expectation of such a calamity, is there? No possibility?"

"I dunno," the officer shrugged. "Except that there is a kind of tip flying around that trouble may come. You know how it is. But tip or not, you gentlemen will have to leave."

"If that's the case…. Come, Fator, and you, Sloman. It seems we are not to have a grandstand seat at this history-making parade after all. Get your coats."

"And don't try to get back either," the policeman offered as a parting shot. "From now till the parade's over, every one of these buildings is being watched. Nobody gets in nor out…."

The roar of the crowd—the roar of that tremendous song—beat now into an empty showroom, a showroom deserted save for the trunk within which a valiant girl lay bound and gagged but jubilant in the knowledge that whatever outrage these men had plotted had been headed off. Had she not been new, very new to the world of intrigue and creeping death she would have wondered uneasily why Garon had given in so easily, why he had seemed almost to expect the order to vacate….

They would come back of course, she thought. They would come back. But what they did to her then would not matter. Nothing would matter if He marched safely down there at the tread of his hosts, marched safely through the singing thousands, the hundreds of thousands who split the welkin with His song:

Never more as soldiers march we on to war.

Murder, loot and rapine know we never more.
Peace and love for all men, calling no one foe,
Beastlike into battle never shall we go.
HEAR US GOD! WE PLEDGE THEE
WAR WE WAGE NO MORE!!!

The chorus roared like the trumpets of Gabriel's host, exploded into a cheer that shook the building, that shook the world itself. He was coming. The Great Man was coming. Up Fifth Avenue he rode, and the clamor that greeted him was like a clashing of firmaments....

IN THE apparently deserted showroom there was a little stir. One of the waxen figures in the window swayed, shaken by the tornado of cheering. No! It wasn't the cheering that moved it. It was moving itself. It was no dummy, it was a man! A man alive, moving now closer to the glass, daring to move closer to the glass because all possible watching eyes were fixed, below there, on the silver-haired, tired-faced man who sat in a slow-moving car and rode with head bowed.

The Great Man was almost directly beneath now. And up here, the seeming dummy was crouching, was lifting in his painted hand an oblong box of black metal to smash it through the glass, to send it hurtling down on the Man and on the crowd below. A bomb to explode in midair, to blast to death the Man Himself and hundreds who shouted now about Him. To blast to death thousands and hundreds of thousands more in the months and years of the holocaust which must follow when those left alive down there would turn from the shambles below and see the gaping hole in the window whence that bomb would come—see the flag waving from a tremendous pole just below that window, the flag of a nation to which Garon and Fator *did not belong!*

The Great Man's car jolted slowly ahead. The assassin's hand lifted a little more. His muscles tightened for the lethal throw, but he waited. Waited till he was sure he could not miss.

"Hold it!" a voice spat behind him.

Something in that voice—a deadly threat—held the killer's hand in momentary paralysis, just long enough for a black-robed figure to leap forward in a great batlike swoop, to grab the death-box in one black-gloved hand, and crash the assassin's skull with the thick-barreled pistol he held in the other.

The pseudo-dummy slumped at the feet of the gray-masked, gray-hatted man. He stood there, that grim figure, for a triumphant moment… twisted at the thud of footsteps from the rear…!

Garon came running across the long floor, Fator. Guns in their hands came up, belched flame. But the black-robed being wasn't where they had aimed. Moving with the speed of black lightning, he had ducked behind a veritable dummy, had leaped to the floor of the showroom and was crouched behind an ornate desk, the box-bomb still in his hand.

"Drop those guns," he whispered, "or I'll throw this at you."

"Throw and be damned," Garon snarled. The two spies had taken covert behind a bronze-fronted showcase. "You might kill us but it will kill you too. We'll all go down to hell together."

THE OTHER crouched lower. His gunhand crept to the side

of the desk. He could not reach them with bullets. He could only hold them there until....

Red Finger pressed the trigger. A vapor spat from the gaping mouth of his gun, shot across the floor, curled around the edge of the case behind which the plotters hid. He shot again and again. There was a thud from the place at which he aimed, another. Dull meaty thuds of unconscious forms hitting the floor.

Red Finger stood up, gingerly placed the bomb on top of the desk that had served for a trench. He did not bother to look at the victims. He knew that they were out of action for hours. It was to the trunk that he stalked, the trunk in which was casketed the girl with the russet hair who shook now with a terrible fear.

She was on her feet, free of the gag and the lashings. She stamped her feet to restore prickling circulation, and gazed wide-eyed at the weird figure who had released her. "Red Finger!" she gasped.

"Forget it," the man rasped harshly. "Forget that you have seen me or who I am. Back there, behind that screen, is a panel. It is where I hid, waiting to find out just what their devil's scheme was. It's from there that Garon and Fator returned to help their killer escape. The staircase goes down into the tunnel which passes under the Plaza to Sixth Avenue. The police forgot about it, as we all knew they would. Get out that way, and get out of the Force. If the cops hadn't come just when they did I would have had to show up then to save you, and they might have succeeded."

"You?" she quavered. "You...."

"I'll follow. But I've got to take that bomb with me. It is more important that all this be covered up than that those fellows be brought to justice. They'll fix up some story that will satisfy the police. The people must never know what happened here. Or that song will be sung no longer. Go. Quickly."

"But—but will I never see you again?"

"Never! I have no right to—GO!" His shout was choked, shaken. It sent her flying out through the door to which he motioned—out of his life…!

THE NEXT morning Ford Duane, sleepy-eyed, languid, unlocked the door of his second-hand bookshop on Fourth Avenue and bent to pick up the mail that had been thrust under it. Circulars. Bills. A small gray envelope addressed in tiny handwriting as clean-cut and beautifully formed as engraving.

Within, a card. "Never say never to a woman." That was all except for the signature. "The Flower."

RED FINGER—SPY POISON!

A MAROON sedan bored steadily into the night, its headlights picking a deserted, narrow road out of the darkness. It was coming from Washington, but it was approaching New York from the north. The Captain of Infantry who drove it had changed its license plates three times since its stealthy departure. He was in civilian clothes, as were his two grizzled, stalwart passengers.

The hat-brims of all three were pulled low over their brows, their coat collars turned up about their jaws to hide their faces even in the auto's dark interior.

The man on the right of the rear seat glanced at the glowing dial of his wristwatch. "Eight-thirty, General," he muttered. "We'll be there in half an hour, right on time. I, for one, will be damned glad of it."

"No more than I, Johnson," his companion growled. "This damned secrecy is nonsensical. Here we are, the commanders of the Coast Defense Forces and the Air Corps, sneaking through our own country like a couple of hunted criminals. One would think we were at war and in enemy territory."

"The Secretary of War's orders, sir. He...."

"The Secretary's an ass! Strictly between ourselves, of course." The speaker swayed as the car started to round a curve that was a dark tunnel through thick set, overhanging trees.

"The Intelligence outfit's balderdash about espionage has him bulldo—" Abrupt brakes cut him off, jarred him forward. The car-horn blared raucously. "What the…?"

"Unlighted car blocking the road, sir," the chauffeur explained crisply. "I'll have to…." Something thumped on the running board. The captain's hand darted to his holstered gun. The door crashed open.

A black figure lurched in, flailed a blackjack against the driver's skull before he could draw his weapon. In the same moment, others, springing masked and shapeless out of the leafy murk, invaded the rear. Muffled shouts, a brief struggle, ended in two meaty thuds. Someone groaned.

"Work quickly," a guttural voice grunted. "We have no time to lose!"

STREET LAMPS made little impression on the gloom of the Fourth Avenue block that is known as the Port of Missing Books. The atmosphere seemed filled with a dusty haze rising from the countless ancient volumes housed in the second-hand bookstores that border its dingy walks.

The drowsy shops were darkened, shut for the night. All but the one whose drab sign read, Duane's Second-Hand Bookstore. Through that one's dirt-encrusted windows a dim luminance still seeped and in its open doorway an alpaca-coated form stood gaunt and tall despite its stoop.

Ford Duane's silhouette was that of an age-wearied man, worn and languid and as nearly ready for the rubbish-heap as the merchandise he purveyed. Had the light fallen across his face it would have been revealed as too young for one who spent his

life in this back-eddy of the Metropolis, its lid-veiled eyes too blue and keen.... Some peculiar quality there was in that furtive keenness. A wary fierceness such as lives in the eyes of a jungle beast that is hunter and hunted at once. There was Death in those eyes. Death which their owner had dealt and would deal again. Death that inevitably would be dealt to him were their ceaseless vigilance even momentarily relaxed.

A strange bookseller? Strange indeed. An unnamed, unnameable soldier in the invisible, endless war that knows no screaming headlines, no marching bands. In the war without glory and without honor whose insidious plot and counterplot endangers an unknowing nation more virulently than even booming cannon and zooming planes.

A shabby derelict of the night shambled past. A distant, single bong vibrated against the city's never-ceasing hum. Duane glanced up at the Consolidated Gas Company's tower clock, hanging like a yellow, figured moon over Fourteenth Street. Eight-thirty. He sighed, turned to go in.

The deep purr of a high-powered motor stopped him, the sough of its brakes. Imperceptibly Duane tensed, came slowly around again to the street. To a sleek limousine from out of which a liveried chauffeur jumped.

The man opened the rear door. The act turned on a light, and made a small, taupe-upholstered room of the car's interior.

"Come here, please." The voice was high-pitched, querulous. An incredibly wrinkled little face peered out at Duane. The old woman was tiny in the big seat, was swathed in funereal silk. An ebony cane diagonaled from seat-edge to floor and the woman's hand gripping it was gray and shriveled like old bone.

Ford Duane's hand, sliding into his trouser pocket, touched metal. He slouched across the sidewalk, halted a foot before he reached the mechanic who stood stiffly at attention, holding open the door. Duane's position was such that he had man and mistress in range of his vision, could act swiftly at any overt move on the part of either.

"Yes, madame," he said quietly. "What can I do for you?"

"You can come nearer," she snapped, her tone that of one used to authority and its exercise. "Do you expect me to shout my business to the town?" Duane saw that there was a flat, square package on the seat beside her. "Pat won't let the door slam on you, if that's what you're afraid of. Will you, Pat?"

"No, ma'am." The man touched an extended finger to his cap visor. "I will not." But Duane didn't hear him. There had been the slightest of slight stresses on the repeated name, *Pat*. A muscle twitched in the bookman's cheek. That name was spelled P-A-T. The three letters had a meaning for him…. His fingers slipped from the automatic in his pocket and he put a foot on the running board, leaning in.

"What is it?" he asked again, loud enough for any possible eavesdropper in the shadows to hear. "You were looking for me?"

"No. I came to New York to see Laroux, the art dealer at the end of the block. But this insane motorcar went mad in Jersey City and by the time Pat brought it to its senses it had made us late. I'm selling the evil thing tomorrow and putting my brougham back into service. That is if there are any decent coach horses left alive. I have a dinner appointment at the Marie Antoinette, I haven't time to go hunting for Laroux. Will you take this landscape and give it to him in the morning?" She jerked her skeleton hand at the package on the seat.

"Gladly." Duane reached for it. "What shall I tell him?"

"To send me a check for it and not rob me too much."

"But who…?"

"Never mind who. He knows who owns Corot's 'Pastorale au Thiers.'" P-A-T again! "Thank you. Good-bye." There was another word, breathed so low Duane was not quite sure he heard it. "Good luck!" And then, high-pitched and peremptory again: "Hurry, Pat. The *Medoc* is too warm already, I'm afraid."

THE LIMOUSINE whispered away. Ford Duane was hesitant for a moment, the wrapped canvas under his arm. He looked up the block at Laroux's art store, as if debating whether to rout him out. He shrugged, shambled, without haste, across the sidewalk into his own shop. He locked the door, left the lights on. Went wearily between the high, gray stacks to the curtained-off backroom that was his living quarters and put the package on a table. From outside half of it was visible, half was hidden by the tied-back drapes behind which Duane slouched.

He whirled, as the portière hid him, went down on his knees. A keen-bladed knife in his hand pried open the end of the flat package that was concealed from out front. Wary that his operations should not move the wrappings, he slid out an unframed canvas, stood up. Any one peering from outside would have been very sure the bundle with which he had been entrusted was untouched.

The picture glowed in the drab light. An ungainly peasant guided a plow through a wheat-field whose every blade was distinct, detailed, as though the master had spent an hour in limning it. Scattered clouds were fleecy, soft in a sun-bright sky.

Duane's lips set in a thin, grim line. He turns again, faces a book-shelved wall. He reaches out, touches a volume, another, a third. The wall moves suddenly on well-oiled hinges, swings back again. There is no one, any longer, in the cubicle with its rumpled camp cot, its gas burner on an up-ended stove, and its hacked table.

In a cramped, windowless cubicle behind that shelved wall Ford Duane clicks on a glaring bulb. He puts the canvas on a narrow ledge jutting from an inner wall. He takes down a bottle from a shelf, wets with its limpid, colorless contents a wad of absorbent cotton. Brushes the soaked fibres across the picture.

A pungent aroma taints the air. In the pictured wheat-field some of the interlaced stalks change color. They make letters, running across the landscape. Faint breath hissed from between Duane's teeth. His eyes blaze suddenly, and as suddenly are veiled.

"Williamsbridge Road," he mutters. "At nine. It will take me an hour—They *were* delayed!"

The volatile compound to which the pastoral had given up its message evaporates. The picture is only a picture again. It is back in its wrappings, that all this time have not moved, and the opening through which it was slid has been repaired. The lights go out in Duane's Bookshop. No one has been seen to go out. But there is no movement in the darkened store. No hint of any presence.

WILLIAMSBRIDGE ROAD runs through the Borough of the Bronx of the City of New York, but its upper reaches are still largely rural. A weathered old house sat far back from the flagstoned sidewalk to which its unkempt lawn sloped and even had its windows not been closely shuttered there were no neighbors to spy on the curious proceedings within it.

"Jane!" A squat, thick-set man with a leonine mane of white hair stopped pacing, suddenly, in a large room inside that house, lit only by a desk lamp near which a girl sat. "What time is it?"

"Half-past eight, Professor." Jane Adams looked up. "They aren't due here till nine." Her tan laboratory cloak did not altogether hide the lissome suppleness of her figure. "We shall just have to wait." Tawny lights glinted in her russet hair. The small oval of her face was lined with fatigue and there were faint blue shadows under her gray eyes.

"Wait!" Kurt Rodney's long, sculptor's fingers plucked nervously at the frayed hem of his stained jacket. "I have waited twenty years. Waited and worked, since the night I stood on a London Street and stared at the bits of scattered flesh and bloody bone that an instant before had been a happy family, mother and father and golden-haired child, strolling the war-darkened pavement. But now that only thirty minutes remain, I can wait no longer!"

"You must be patient."

"I don't know why it is that this fever possesses me now," the old man ran on. "A fever of dread. Of fear. *Fear!* Till you came to my laboratory at the University and persuaded me to take myself and my apparatus into hiding I did not know what that word meant. There was only my spectroscopes, and my dynamometers, and the joy of discovering hitherto unknown forces. You made me ask for Sabbatical leave. You made me board the Around-the-World liner and then sneak ashore again in disguise. You made me come here to this benighted hide-away and remain here a prisoner—for six months."

"For your sake—and for our country's sake, Professor." There was compassion in Jane's tone, and firmness. "If the secret of what you were doing, have done, were to be learned by America's enemies…?"

"They would use it against her and my work would be in vain,"

Rodney broke in. "Yes. I know. That was why I consented. Excuse me, Jane. I am a silly old man." An endearing smile of apology seemed to light up the craggy, seamed countenance.

"You are a very great scientist, and a greater humanitarian. You have saved our cities, their teeming millions, from the nightmare horrors of the inevitable Next War. When the Army officers see what you have devised, when you demonstrate it to them…."

"Jane! Suppose something is wrong! Suppose it doesn't work. They will laugh at me…."

"It will work. A hundred times it has worked. There's no reason why…."

"Let's try it again. We have time. We must make sure."

"Very well." The girl lifted, wearily, moved to a wall. A click and the chamber was flooded with light.

A HUGE cage centered the room, a cage of mosquito screening. Its floor was covered by a miniature hamlet, tiny houses row on row along inch-wide streets. Surrounding the toy village, green-painted paper-maché simulated rolling country. Studding the line where town and country met were a number of small metal contrivances, curiously intricate. They might be models of field guns, except that the wee barrels were mounted on boxes out of whose surfaces quarter-inch glass lenses glittered. Thread-like, insulated wires connected these, coiled out through the wire meshes to a rheostat on a nearby cluttered table that in turn was joined to a wall-plug by a metal-covered cable.

On one wall of the cage, just beneath its roof, a row of inch-square cages of the same wire netting were fastened. Within each one a common house-fly preened itself, and each tiny cage was provided with a small door that could be opened from outside to make its occupant free in the larger chamber.

Rodney peered down into the cage. "Nonsensical, this display," he growled. "Unscientific."

"But practical. The men who are coming here will be more impressed by it than by all your careful graphs and charts." Jane gestured to the black face of a closed safe recessed into the further wall. "They are practical men, not theorists."

"Perhaps! Let us start!"

The girl moved the rheostat handle, from switch-point to switch-point. Stopped it half-way of its arc. A vague, humming sound was perceptible. That was all, but it seemed to fill the room with tenseness, with a spine-prickling excitement. Professor Rodney's gray face grew paler, his lips colorless.

"All right," he said. "Go ahead."

Jane stepped to the cage, lifted one of the small doors. The fly inside stopped preening itself. The girl tapped a sharp finger against the wire and the insect took wing.

It circled momentarily, darted over Toytown. Darted *towards* Toytown. The tiny gun-tubes came alive, jerked upward, spat minuscule, shiny pellets. The almost microscopic projectiles struck the fly, fell with it to the cage floor.

"Perfect," Rodney exclaimed. "If that had been an enemy airplane, or a fleet of them, raiding the city by day or night, the infra-red rays would have aimed and shot the rifles at them, and destroyed them with the same efficiency. No matter how high they flew, no matter how silently. Our cities are safe from poison gas, from bombs. The same devices on our own planes, battleships, tanks, will make their marksmanship perfect. I have made America invincible."

"Invincible! And have insured peace." There was elation in the girl's face, overpowering joy. "Professor Rodney! You…!"

A knock at the outside door checked her. It came again. There was a pause. Then the double rap was repeated.

"They're here," the scientist gasped.

"At last!"

JANE ADAMS almost ran out of the room, into the small foyer that separated it from the entrance. In moments she was back, behind her two tall, military-appearing men whose hat-brims were pulled low over their brows, whose coat collars were turned up to screen their faces.

The newcomers looked curiously at the astonishing contrivance in the center of the room. Then one turned.

"Professor Rodney?" His voice was hoarse, guttural.

"Yes. I am Kurt Rodney. And you are…?"

"Generals Sloane and Johnson of the United States Army. You have some device here you wish to sell to the War Department."

"No!"

"What do you mean? We were ordered here to…."

"Not to sell. To give to the nation. Gentlemen! As you know, there is no question that any future declaration of war will at once he accompanied by air raids on civilian centers of population."

"There is no doubt of that. The next war will be directed

113

against the non-belligerent populations of the adversary countries. It will be a holocaust...."

"It will not. I have destroyed that fear for the United States for once and always."

"Interesting—if true."

The physicist's face darkened with anger. "You doubt me? Here is the proof." He thumped the huge cage. "Here." The disturbed flies buzzed.

"Yes?"

"Yes." Rodney thrust a hand inside the breast-opening of his jacket, struck his familiar lecture posture. "My device is based on the principle of the photoelectric cell that is used in industry to open doors, stop and start machinery, inspect and throw out imperfect products, and so on. You are familiar with it. Yes?"

"Yes."

"But I utilize the invisible infra-red rays, which have a penetrative power far beyond that of visible light. Searching the sky with these, despite darkness or fog, my invention can...."

"Professor!" the girl broke in. "Just a minute." She was at the safe-door, had been manipulating its silvery dial, but had not opened it. Her hand remained on its knob.

"Er—what is it, Jane? Why do you interrupt me?"

"You've forgotten to ask these gentlemen for their credentials. After all, we have only their word for their identity."

GENERAL JOHNSON laughed, humorlessly. "Of course. Here they are." He brought a leather folder out of his pocket, flipped it open. Rodney peered near-sightedly at it. The seal of the United States was embossed across its lines of printing and writing, across a pasted photograph of the man who held it.

"This seems to be correct, Jane." He muttered. "I have no doubt this gentleman is whom he represents himself to be."

"General Johnson!" The girl seemed not yet to be satisfied. "How high does an eagle fly?"

"How high…?" The man stopped. A sudden, brittle silence shut down. Then there was a gun in his hand, shouting at the girl. "You are too smart for your own good, young lady." The other man's automatic, too, was out, was covering the professor. "You caught me with that password question but that will not prevent us from getting what we came for."

Jane twirled the safe knob, stepped away from it. "I didn't catch you with that question. The real General Johnson would not have known the answer and would have said so. There isn't any answer." She smiled grimly. "What betrayed you is the shoes you both are wearing, but I had to make sure."

"The shoes…! They're dress shoes of the United States army. Regular issue. We were careful about that as about everything else."

"Too careful. Generals in the American army purchase their own shoes. They are the same as any civilian's. Yours…."

"You're an ass, Gorslum." The putative General Sloane, silent till now, darted a vicious glare at his comrade. "But we're wasting time. The plans are in that safe. Open it, girl."

The corners of Jane's mouth twitched. "And if I don't?"

"You will." There was no suavity in his accents, only a hissing threat the more horrible because of its low tone. "We have ways of making you and they are not—pleasant."

"Very well." The girl shrugged. She turned, manipulated the combination dial. The painted steel swung open—and a mass of charred, smoldering ashes spilled out. "If you can make anything out of these you're good," Jane chuckled. "That last flip I gave the knob detonated a little bomb in here that I set for action while Professor Rodney was starting his lecture."

"You witch!" Gorslum exclaimed. He sprang forward, slammed the side of his gun against the girl's cheek, gashing it. "You she-devil…!"

The blow jolted the girl backward, against the table on which the rheostat rested. Her elbow struck the rheostat-handle, jammed it against the terminal marked, "HIGH." Sparks coruscated from the miniature field-guns within the cage and the little boxes glowed cherry-red, white. Melted down into shapeless lumps.

"And that finishes the last trace of Kurt Rodney's secret," Jane Adams gritted, through teeth clamped on the pain of her wound. "He knows now why I insisted on supplying the rig-up with far more current than it could safely take."

"Jane," the old man groaned. "Jane. You are wiser than I. Far wiser.…"

"Destroyed the secret, eh!" Gorslum was white-faced with wrath, but his thick mouth was tight and very cruel. "*Has* she destroyed the secret, Trano?"

THE OTHER man licked dry lips with a pink tongue. "She has not. It still lives—in its creator's brain." And then the two men moved, quickly, purposefully, as though at an unspoken signal. When they were through both the Americans were in chairs, lashed and helpless. "He will tell us, and be glad to tell us," Trano continued, as though nothing had intervened, "all about it before we are done with him."

"Never." Rodney had come out of his daze. "I will die before I speak. He was somehow majestic, bound as he was, somehow awesome. "And my invention will die with me."

The sound Trano made might have been intended for a laugh, but the girl shuddered at its evil implication. "You will pray for death, my dear professor," he lipped. "You will think death a blessing."

"Stop the talk and get to work." Gorslum seemed anxious, jittery. "I don't want to keep that car standing out there overlong. We hid those we took it from well enough, but there is always the chance that they may be found and an alarm broadcast."

"They will not be found," the other grinned, horribly. "And if they are, they will not talk. I changed our friends' instructions slightly. For the better, as you now understand. But...." He paused. "Ah! The professor has been good enough to provide me with just what I need."

He darted to the table, snatched up an electric soldering-iron. "This develops a quite satisfactory degree of heat." He thumbed its switch, watched its swollen end grow dull black, glisten, begin to turn cherry-red. He turned, prowled toward Rodney, the long cord trailing behind him. "Take off his shoes."

Gorslum knelt, fumbled at the scientist's laces. Jane watched him with dilated pupils, but oddly enough the expression of her eyes was not quite hopeless. She seemed to be listening, intently. Not to any sound in the room. Not to any sound that existed. Her gaze flickered away from the ominous group around the other chair, flitted to the shutter-blinded window....

And was pulled back by a piercing scream of agony from Rodney's writhing mouth. By the acrid tang of burned flesh.

The scream died down to a moan. "Are you ready to talk?" Gorslum questioned. "Or shall my friend proceed?"

The professor's blue lips quivered. He was an old man, Jane thought. How much could he endure? Was he breaking? Already?

"May you both... go to Hell!" From him, from the cloistered scientist, it was not a meaningless oath but a malediction and a terrible curse. *"To Hell...!"* And then he was screaming again, was writhing in anguish. The pungent smell of charred meat was nauseating....

The flies were buzzing, excitedly, in their cages. They smelled carrion, battered their wings against the wire, avid to get at it. Nausea retched at the girl's stomach, thrust dizzy tentacles into her brain. The shrill sound of Rodney's agony beat dully against her swimming ears. It stopped. A guttural voice was incoherent, meaningless....

It ended in a splintering crash—and a sudden silence. A silence that cleared Jane's vision for her, that brought her back to realization of her surroundings.

THE TWO spies were frozen, statuesque, Gorslum holding Rodney's bare ankles, Trano on his knees, the soldering-iron in his white-knuckled hand. The window-shutter was splintered, its aperture gaping. Someone was surging in through it. Some-one—or *something!* The formless bulk that dropped lithely to the floor was a swirling mass of dark draperies, a black and grisly phantasm. It thudded on the wood, straightened.

"God!" Gorslum gulped. "Red Finger!"

The apparition was tall, draped in a long black cloak that obliterated its figure. A gray felt hat crowned it, and a gray mask made it faceless except for narrow slits behind which there was a blue, dangerous glitter. But that which made of it a macabre, fantastic threat was the hand that jabbed a revolver point-blank at the torturers. Black, that hand was, black gloved. Except for one finger, the finger that curled around the weapon's trigger. That was a glaring scarlet as if it had been dipped in fresh blood.

"Yes. Red Finger!" The masked head nodded and the toneless acknowledgment seemed to savor the dread that name inspired among all who moved in the murky underworld of international intrigue. "You forgot that New York is my district, Gorslum and Trano. Or did you think that you could succeed where so many others have failed?"

The only answer was a whimper from a clamped throat, a whimper of deadly fear. These men were brave. None but the brave enlist in the invisible war. But the man who stood before them was a whispered legend among their like a tradition of supernatural invincibility and relentless doom.

"Stand up!"

Gorslum dropped the professor's ankles. Trano straightened, slowly—exploded into lightning action that flung the heated iron he held straight at Red Finger's eye-slits.

The glove-held gun spat orange-yellow flame. The glowing iron clanged, smashed, in mid-air, into a hundred pieces that clattered down. But the momentary diversion had given the spies time to snatch out their own guns.

The sound of firing was continuous thunder in the room. Fiery jets laced the air. A lax body thudded down. Lead plucked at black cloth, sliced a fluttering fragment from it. A second body hung limply on the wire-mesh cage, sprayed a scarlet rain on Toytown.

Red Finger swayed, clutched at the window-sill for support. He hung there for a long moment. A darker patch spread, glistening, on the dark cloth of his cloak, at his side. He fumbled at the fluttering drapes and his gun was gone.

He was coming across the floor to the girl who called herself Jane Adams. He was *staggering* across the floor, clutching at the table, at a chair-back, to keep from falling. He got to her, fumbled at the knots that tied her.

HE WAS mumbling low words to her. "I got here as quickly as I could. The message was delayed."

"I told you I would see you again."

Her tone too, was low. But Kurt Rodney would not have heard them had they shouted. He had fainted. "When you sent me out of that office on Fifth Avenue and out of your life, I told you never to say never to a woman."

"Flower!" Recognition seemed to give him new life, to staunch his wound. "You! Who are you, Flower? Who...?"

"Number six-one-three. Just a number, Red Finger, to the Force. But to you?"

"A girl who has no business in the Force. Get out, Flower. Get out before it's too late. Before a bullet finds its billet in your soft, sweet body. Or worse happens to it. *Worse....*"

"And you, Red Finger?"

"I—I stay."

"Then I stay, too. Red Finger! Are we neither of us to know life? Are we...?"

He was gone from her. He was across the room, at the window. She tried to rise, but she was still held light by the lashings he had not finished unfastening.

"It will take you a minute to free yourself." He was out of the window. "Will you ever free me?" He vanished into the chilly night, without waiting for an answer.

A WEEK later Ford Duane, still weak and pale from the automobile accident that had sent him to a certain private and very discreet sanitarium in the Bronx, unlocked his bookshop. Among the litter of letters and bills that had been poked through the slit in this door during his absence was a russet rose. Impaled on its stem was a narrow slip of paper, and on that paper one word:

"*Never!*"

LOCKED IN WITH DEATH

ISOLATED BY some accident of time and tide from the rushing currents of the vast ocean that is New York, a certain drab block on Fourth Avenue is a doldrum of stagnation. Here Time moves slowly, if at all. Here dust stirred up in busier streets sifts down to film sidewalk cases that wistfully offer tattered books to browsers who look but seldom buy. Here gray, drowsy men are content to dawdle undisturbed in their grimy shops that are derelict as the rotting wrecks in Neptune's graveyard of forgotten ships.

Life moves slowly in this back-eddy of the seething metropolis, and Death seems to have passed it by—except in one dingy cubicle—and there Death is a livid, almost tangible presence.

Ford Duane's Second-Hand Bookstore is no different, even to the most observant eye, from other berths of this port of missing books. Most deliberately it is no different in appearance from the shop of Radley Ransom on its left or that of Lazare Garreau on its right. But the shadows that lie heavily between its high stacks of dogeared volumes are the shadows of fear, and the quiet that broods in its dimness is the hush of an omnipresent dread.

One late afternoon Ford Duane stood, gawky and stooped, in the door of his shop. His shabby alpaca smock hung loosely on his lank frame, so that it seemed painfully, almost cadaverously thin, and heavy grooves were graven deep into his gaunt, expressionless countenance.

Duane's face was evasively youthful for this abode of the aged and weary. Yet his eyelids were slitted as though the effort to raise them were too great and every line of him drooped with bone weariness…. Concealed by the lackadaisical folds of his gray apparel there was slender strength—muscles like steel springs, hairtrigger nerves that could instantaneously command those muscles to lightning-like action. Behind those lowered lids, eyes of the keenest blue were eternally restless, eternally watchful. That leashed power, that unrelenting vigilance, was the price of Ford Duane's safety—and the safety of a nation!

Hunter and hunted, stalker and stalked, Duane was far more than he seemed. There was a price on his head in more than one chancellery, but in a certain secret room in the nation's capital he was a number, and a name quite different from that which the tarnished letters on the streaked plate glass above him spelled out.

Ford Duane turned smoothly to a whistle that lilted along the street. His furtive look flicked to the whistler, and a muscle that had twitched along the ridge of his sharp jaw relaxed. It was only a grimy-faced boy in the dark blue of a telegraph company who was approaching.

The messenger-boy glanced at a sheaf of white and blue envelopes in his hand, glanced up at Duane's window. Stopped.

"Yuh Ford Duane?" the youngster asked.

"Yes. I'm Duane."

"Postal—ah—Telegraph. Got a message fer yuh. Postal—ah—Telegraph."

THE PHRASING was awkward. The pause between the two words of the name was awkward…. A pulse pumped in Ford Duane's wrist.

"All right. Let me have it." There was nothing in the bookman's voice to betray his sudden agitation. But behind his untroubled brow his thoughts were whirring. *P*ostal—*ah*—*T*elegraph. It had been repeated, making three words out of what should have been two. Three words whose initials were, P—A—T!

"Sign here."

Duane signed the book P-A-T. Those initial letters were a signal. Now and again they had been cryptically embodied in a peddler's cry, a street singer's appeal, a society dame's querulous berating of her chauffeur. They meant something to Ford Duane. They meant action, and danger…. Death! Surely for someone. Perhaps—for him!

"Here's yuhr telegram." The boy handed it over, turned away.

"Wait!" Duane's command had halted him. "Wait a minute." The book vendor was fumbling in his pocket for a tip, but his hand stayed there. There was startlement in the gray eyes that had sought his face. A sudden darkening in them. Of fear? No. Not fear, but some other obscure emotion. A lock of hair protruding from under the blue, red-braided cap was tawny.

"Flower!" Ford Duane's exclamation was low-toned as he put a coin in an extended palm that was too white, too soft to be

an urchin's. "Flower! I told you to get out of the game. It's too dangerous for a...."

"T'anks!" The messenger had whirled again, and was striding down the street. Duane dared not run after her....

There is one army in which a woman can serve as well as a man. It is a wraithlike army that secretly wages a war that never ends; a war of underground strategy; of silent, unsung heroisms; of trickery and deceit; in which triumphs go unrewarded and the participants fail only once.

Because they must remain unknown to their antagonists, the soldiers of that secret army must be unknown to one another. That is the rule of the game. But they are human, nevertheless, and sometimes a mask slips, a disguise is penetrated. They are human, and

though it is far better that they should not, they sometimes have human emotions.

The telegram was clutched in Ford Duane's right hand. His left pressed furtively against the breast pocket of his smock. Something crackled under that pressure, as dried petals crackle, and a vague fragrance came from it, the perfume of a russet rose. Weeks before that rose had been a wordless message from a comrade whose name he did not even know—except that he called her Flower!

They are very human, the men and women who are phantom fighters in a phantom war.

"Bad news, Duane?" a voice asked, rustling and sere as dead leaves. Radley Ransom peered at him out of rheumy eyes. The old man had shuffled over from his own stall. White-bearded and senile, the only emotion left to him was curiosity. "Taint often any of us gets a telegram."

"I don't know, haven't read it yet." Ford ripped open the blue and white envelope, pulled out the sheet it contained. "No. Looks like a business message. I've been doing a little special trading lately for a couple of collectors. This is from one of them."

Ransom made shift to get a view of the telegram. "Sure is a long one," he mumbled, and doddered away. Time was, he ruminated, when he too had hopes of building up a trade among bibliophiles. There was money in it.

Duane's thin lips were touched by the hint of a grim smile. This was a simple code, and effective because it was simple. Who would suspect the garrulous communication to be other than it seemed?

126

ADAMS SAYS THACKERAY ROMANCES OFFERED
FOR SALE PROVIDED OFFER TENDERED TODAY
STOP EVERHARD DESIRES ACQUIRE THEM FOR
OSTLEY STOP UNDERTAKES REWARD TRADER
WITH OFFENBACH'S THUCYDIDES EDITED
NATIONAL ACADEMY STOP VIGILANTLY EXERT
EFFORTS INCLUDE NORTON VELLUM EDITION
SOCRATES THEMES STOP IMPERATIVE GET
AHEAD TOM EVERHARD STOP

PAYTON A. THOMPSON

He read it again. Then his slender, strong fingers crumpled it
and tossed it into the gutter. If there were, somewhere unseen, a
stealthy observer spying upon him that gesture would convince
him of the utter unimportance of the paper.

The second reading had hold Duane all he need know. Disre-
garding the punctuation, the "stops," he had read only the first
letters of each word of the message;

ASTROFSPOTTEDATFOURTWOTENAVEEINVES-
TIGATEPAT

and then had separated them into new words:

ASTROF SPOTTED AT FOUR-TWO-TEN AVE E.
INVESTIGATE. PAT.

Ford Duane straightened a pile of coverless *National
Geographic Magazines* in a box trestled in front of his store,
adjusted a jagged-edged cardboard sign that said; YOUR
CHOICE, FIVE CENTS. A vagrant breeze flapped pages

of one of the magazines, a title struck at him—"Lemuria: The Friendly Land."

Duane's thin lips twitched with secret, grim amusement. Yes, they were very friendly to tourists, the Orientals of Lemuria. They showed visitors their miniature gardens, their quaint houses, and smilingly sold them tawdry gimcracks in their picturesque bazaars. But in carefully guarded harbors were shipyards seething with activity. In mountain fortresses death lurked for those who dared to penetrate cuff-walled plateaus covered by acre upon acre of factories where steel was being fashioned into cannon, brass into shells, and fuming acids with bales of fleecy cotton made into merchandise of Hell. These things the tourists did not see.

Friendly, were they, the Lemurians? Smilingly they looked at Occidental Nations riven by dissension, weakened by long poverty, glaring at each other with hatred. Only America was still strong in the Western World. Only America still stood in the way of the scheme for terrestrial empire that brooded behind those smiling, saffron faces.

Still smiling, Lemurian fishermen cast their seines, *and their sounding lines,* off America's coast. Still smiling, Lemurian students conned books in American universities, and conned the American mind. Lemurian artisans labored in America's factories, attended meetings of workers, permeated every tiny vein and pulsing artery of American life. Smilingly, always smilingly, they sought out the secret of American strength—and the vulnerable spot every strength must possess.

So vast a network of espionage must have a single head. That head was the man known in the hidden chronicles of the secret war as Konyl Astrof. And if Astrof was in America, the Lemurians had found the weakness they sought. Their smiles were tightening into snarling, menacing grins!

The blue and white paper already mucked by the mire of the Fourth Avenue gutter put it squarely up to Ford Duane to wipe those grins from the saffron countenances of the Lemurian War Lords!

Gray dusk settled on Fourth Avenue from a leaden sky. "I'm shutting up early, Radley," Duane called to his ancient neighbor. "I'll have to get busy if I want to earn that commission. Everhard is a tough man to buck."

THE STREET designated by the name of Avenue E is only two blocks long, cutting across the East River shore of Manhattan Island. Some decades-long litigation, some defect in title, dragging a weary way through weary courts, have kept it in a state of arrested development; so that the brick warehouses lining it are unoccupied, their windows boarded up, their doors fastened by rusty padlocks.

Forty-two-ten Avenue E was cloaked in the fog that rolled oilily up from the River to make a dark, blind gut of the forgotten thoroughfare. The old warehouse might have been a tomb in some cemetery of giants for all the animation that was apparent behind its slime-sweating front.

One by one, three vague forms slid through the fog, seeming almost a part of it, so little sound did their movements make. One by one they vanished into the gloom-shrouded embrasure of forty-two-ten's high, unlighted portal.

No key could possibly have turned in the rusted padlock holding the great door closed. But there was a furtive scrape of wood on wood. Momentarily an oblong showed, blacker against the vertical black. And once more the niche was empty, and silent.

Slithering footsteps whispered within the stygian vastness of the ancient warehouse. A door softly shut. The sounds of furtive movement descended. Another door opened and shut. The darkness was close, and heavy with fungoid damp, with the fetid miasma of a catacomb. Breaths hissed. A scratch rasped the silence.

A match flame spurted into being, low down. A lamp wick was edged with red glow, blossomed into steady light. The luminescence filled a small windowless vault and cast monstrous, brooding shadows up against the ceiling. The bare earthen floor was greasy and black with the seepage from the sewers that lay in their long graves close against the structure's foundations.

The man who had lit the lamp on the floor straightened. His shadow heaved above him, like some gargantuan, black creature of doom to whom light was a curse.

His mask was a wide, black bar across his face, but the ponderous, blunt jaw it did not hide; the square-sided, bony cheeks were eloquent of power, of an intellectual strength whose physical counterpart was manifest in his bull shoulders and columnar massiveness of frame. His mouth was thick-lipped, sensuous—sadistic.

The diminutive stature of the masked couple whom he confronted contrasted grotesquely with his bulk. A door of unpainted wood newly set into the wall framed them; and they were wiry as weasels, shrewd, cruel. A saffron tinge overlay what little of their skin that was exposed. Their pointed fingernails were tainted with a pallid blue cast. Those nails were like talons, like claws fashioned to tear quivering flesh.

"You are certain that you were unobserved coming here?" The big man held his voice low, but it boomed in the confined space. "Absolutely certain?"

TWO YELLOW heads bobbed in assent as inhaled breath hissed between teeth startlingly white.

"Good. This is the last time I shall use this rendezvous. It would have been unfortunate had some carelessness of yours betrayed it. Unfortunate for you." Even under the saffron complexion of his hearers a sharp paleness was visible, a pallor of fear at the reptilian menace chilling the measured statement.

"The reports that have been brought here to me have been satisfactory. The transcontinental railroads have been mined, our men are posted at the strategic points to cut all telephone and telegraph cables, the static-producing radio stations are set up and ready to blanket the air. Our transport fleets are within striking distance of the American Coast. It is you two who will flash the signal that will disrupt the American communications and give our forces time to do their part. You will do that at midnight, Eastern Standard Time, tomorrow. At midnight. Do not fail. With five uninterrupted hours in which to work, the Lemurian armies will be firmly entrenched at a dozen strategic points on the continent, and the flag of the Setting Moon will never be dislodged from its soil.

"Go now, and do not fail. For the Emperor."

"For the Emperor," the Lemurians intoned, making the curious gesture that from time immemorial has signified utter abasement, utter devotion to their ruler who, legend says, has descended straight from the God of the Night. They turned....

Before they could reach the door it flew open. For an instant the aperture was a blank, staring orifice of black threat, and then a grisly apparition materialized within it.

"Not so fast, my friends," a sepulchral voice intoned. "Not so fast."

That voice was muffled by a gray mask that made the speaker faceless under a gray mask save for narrow slits through which blue menace glittered. Swirling black draperies cloaked the immensely tall figure, making it shapeless, ominous. But that from which the Lemurians fell back in deathly terror, that which froze their leader to a motionless statue of dismay—was the hand from which jutted a thick-barreled pistol.

That hand was black as midnight, black as the lustreless draperies from which it protruded, except for one grim, blood-red finger that curled about the trigger.

A gasp from the big man broke the brittle silence. "Red Finger! *Bozhe moi!* Red... Finger!"

The face of him who stood in the doorway could not be seen, but he seemed to smile, forebodingly. "Red Finger, Astrof," the toneless voice murmured. "You should have remembered me when you planned to take over the United States."

Astrof forced a smile to his colorless lips, a smile that had no humor. "How could I forget, Red Finger? One after another you have ended the careers of the best spies the world has ever known. One after another they have failed, and when the question was asked—why?—the answer always came whispered back, Red Finger. When I worked for the Tsar, you defeated me. When I moved on to espionage service of one, then of another nation, always you defeated me. Your name is the dread and the despair of all international intrigue. I should not have forgotten you when I advised my latest employers that I could conquer America. *And I did not!*"

The last words snapped like a whip, and like a whip a noose lashed down over Red Finger's head from behind, jerked taut to clamp his arms to his sides. Yellow fingers flailed to smash the thick-barreled gun from the black-gloved hand with the carmine forefinger. Diminutive Lemurians, three of them, swarmed over the counter-spy, bringing him down.

Astrof's big-chested laugh roared out, echoing in the gloomy depths of the old warehouse. "I did not forget you, Red Finger," he chuckled when that laugh ended. "I thought very carefully about you. And—cleverly. No, my friend? For years I have studied tales that were whispered about you. I learned that only one person knew who you were when you doffed that somewhat spectacular masquerade of yours, the little man in the secret room in Washington. I learned that you were only called upon for action when the most feared of international spies were at work.

"Many men have gone after you and failed. I decided that I should make you come after me. So, my friend, I carefully allowed myself to be discovered entering this place. Who greater than Astrof could Red Finger send to defeat? And I made a little speech that would be sure to bring you into the open, thinking that you must act at once to save that pig's country of yours from disaster. Then—my men who were hidden took you unawares."

"What are you going to do with me?" Red Finger's captors no longer held him. But they had wrapped the rope around him so that only his head protruded from its coils, like the head of a chrysalis emerging from its cocoon.

"Do? Start now to build the set-up you heard me describe. But first," the chuckling triumph was gone from Astrof's speech, "so that I may be certain of its success, I shall—kill you!"

EVEN THAT did not break the American's stoic calm. "It was bound to come sooner or later. You might as well be the one."

The Russian's big hands fisted, opened. Closed again. "Scheming to the last, Red Finger? Thinking that when your body, knifed, shot, drowned, is found, the hounds of your law will be let loose on Astrof. And though he is too clever to be caught he will be harried, his work rendered impossible. But you do not know how cunning is the man who has at last brought you low." He snapped an unintelligible word in Lemurian.

The little yellow men went out. Red Finger heard their small feet patter away through the darkness. He was alone with his enemy. "Well?" he asked.

Astrof stared at him, a slow, foreboding smile creeping across his heavy face. A long moment of silence dragged. Then, "Listen," he said. "Listen."

Silence again. Silence that was broken by the rapid tick, tick;

tick, tick of a clock. It was somewhere in this room. Somewhere in the black shadows under its vaulted ceiling. Tick, tick; tick, tick.

"You hear it, Red Finger? One of my colleagues has switched on an infernal machine, a bomb, set within a recess where the keystones of these arches join. It will explode in ten minutes. You see, my friend, this warehouse is supported on a series of arches like these, each crossed, two holding up the others. When one pair falls they all fall, and the building will fall. When Red Finger is found, if ever he will be, the little man in the room at Washington will be sorry, very sorry, that he sent his ace into an empty building where no one was, and that his ace was caught by the collapse of that building.

"And now, *au revoir*. I will see you again—in that Hell where all spies go."

Astrof launched into movement, quicker than his huge body seemed capable of. He stooped, snatched up a loose end of the rope that bound Red Finger, lurched out of the exit. The door slammed shut, pounding solidly into its jamb. The bound man heard a bar scrape down across it on the other side, another! He saw that the rope the spy-master had taken with him passed through an angled nick that had been cut in the door's edge.

And then the rope was snaking through that hole. It tightened, pulled at him. It rolled him over and over, unwinding from his body. It was gone.

Battered, dizzy from the giddy revolutions, Red Finger lay half-dazed against the door. Astrof was not to be caught napping. He had taken the rope with him so that when Red

Finger's smashed corpse was found in the debris of a structure fallen by its own weight, no suspicion of any human agency in his death would arise in the minds of his finders.

Tick, tick; tick, tick.

The rapid little clicking sounds pattered against the welter in the counterspy's throbbing brain. Tick, tick; tick, tick. Each tiny click clipping a half-second from his life.

No! Realization exploded him to his feet. His work was not ended, could not be ended. Astrof was free, to consummate his plans for America's destruction. Astrof was free, and the shrewd saboteur himself had said that Red Finger was the only one who could defeat him. Red Finger could not die. Red Finger dared not die.

Tick, tick; tick, tick. The Lemurians had searched him as they bound him, had left him nothing, absolutely nothing with which to break out of here. He hurled himself at the mocking, resinous wood of the door. It hurled him back, staunch, immovable. It was inches thick. The bars that Astrof had let down across it made it a part of the wall itself. Till that wall fell Red Finger's cell was inescapable. It would fall soon enough, but that would be too late.

Tick, tick; tick, tick. How much time had passed? How much time was there still to go?

The bomb was up there, where the arches joined in a point. If he could reach it. If he could only reach it. There was nothing to stand upon. The walls were rough, grooved where powdered mortar had sifted out from between the old bricks. Red Finger ripped off his gloves, dug frantic finger nails into one such groove. A brick grated, slid out. He shoved a toe into the niche it left, dug out another.

Tick, tick; tick, tick.

He was halfway up the wall. It curved out and upward. He gained a foot, another foot. Reached a shaking hand to pry at a new brick….

And fell, pounding hard into the black muck that floored this lethal chamber! He was no fly. He had no suckers on his feet, his hands, with which to cling upside down to a ceiling that otherwise gave no hold. He rolled, scrambled to hands and knees. Lifted erect. Time must be almost up. He would meet death upright.

Tick, tick; tick, trsssssk. The sound was changing. It was blurring, rasping. Was the ten minutes up?

That rasping sound was not from above. It was from outside the door. It was the scrape of the bars against the door, that was moving—swinging outward!

The swinging door uncovered a slim, boyish form… in the blue uniform of a telegraph messenger.

"Flower!" Red Finger ejaculated, and literally hurled himself toward her. "Flower! Come on. Run. Run!"

"They're gone! It's all…."

He reached her, swept her up in his arms, not pausing in his stride as he hurtled toward the stairs down which he had crept, thinking himself unobserved. "All right be damned," he grunted. "The building's coming down." He was flying up those stairs, winged by a terror that somehow had redoubled with the presence of the girl. But even in his terrible haste, his terrible fear, he knew that the body in his arms was warm, and soft, and very dear. "They set a bomb and it may go off at any moment."

A GASP answered him, and the girl he knew as Flower shuddered against him. He had reached the upper floor, was leaping, vaulting in desperate effort to attain the rear window he had jimmied to gain entrance.

"How did you get here? How on earth did you find me?" Red Finger asked the question, not knowing if death would let her answer him.

"I read the telegram, hid near here. I was—afraid—for you."

"You read…." Here was the window! He thrust her through it, vaulted out: She was a slim, phantom figure running alongside him through the dark alley. She was— They were out in the street. Red Finger twisted to a shadowy, cubical bulk in the fog, far down the block. An auto. He sprinted toward it.

"I thought so," he gritted. "Astrof would wait to laugh when the building went down. That's how he's built."

A crash, tumultuous, earth-shaking, obliterated speech. Dust rolled around him. Choking, spluttering, he lunged out of the cloud, groping toward the auto. A pallid oval was a face goggling out of a black roadster's front seat, ten feet away.

"Astrof!" Red Finger yelled.

Orange-red flame jetted at him. Leaden spray from a blazing gun. Red Finger left the ground in a tremendous leap. His heels pounded on a moving runningboard. He lay across the roadster's half-door and his fingers clutched the gun. Astrof had not time to fire again, wrenched it out of the hand that held it.

Astrof was strong, powerful. But Hercules himself could not have resisted the lethal fury that inflamed Red Finger.

The gun crashed against Konyl Astrof's temple. The Russian's gigantic bulk slumped unconscious in the driver's seat. A police whistle shrilled, far-off. Red Finger grabbed the steering wheel of the roadster, which in the lightning instant of that brief fight had been slowly gathering speed, twirled it. The car made a half circle in the roadway. Red Finger pushed down on a lax knee. The car leaped into sudden speed. At the final moment the counter-spy leaped from its running board and the black car crashed thunderously into the huge pile of shattered brick on which the dust raised by its collapse had not yet started to settle.

The policeman, coming on the run around the corner, saw a tall, slender man staring at the piled ruins of a condemned ware-house that had fallen at last and at the mangled wreck of a road-ster that had smashed into it. "God," Ford Duane jerked out as the patrolman came up. "The damn fool. He almost dipped me, speeding a mile a minute. He must have been drunk, or crazy."

"Drunk, I guess." The officer grunted, fighting off the shock of what he saw with a mechanical functioning of routine. "Comin' from some damn masquerade, mebbe. Looka what fell out o' the car." He held out black, torn fabric to Duane. "Musta been dressed up like a Ku Klux Klanner or somethin'...." He broke off. Then—"Godfrey! I wunner if anyone was caught under there. I got to 'phone headquarters." He lumbered off.

Was anyone else caught under there? Was anyone...? The blood in Ford Duane's veins were suddenly cold. Had *she* won free of the falling brick? There was no living soul, beside himself and the flatfoot in the street....

And then the forefront of a crowd surged around the corner. Before he was asked what he had been doing in deserted Avenue E, Fort Duane must slip away. He reeled as he walked, as though he were half-dazed. As though the fog had seeped into his bones with the chill of death.

RADLEY RANSOM was just dragging his sidewalk stands into his store for the night as Ford Duane passed him. "Oh, Duane," he called.

"Yes." The younger man's voice was toneless, tortured. "What is it, Ransom?"

"This telegram came for you 'bout ten minutes ago. I signed for it."

Duane snatched the envelope from him, ripped it open with shaking fingers. It said:

*S*ALE *T*UESDAY *I*NSTEAD STOP *L*ET *L*AYTON *I*NCLUDE *N*EWTON'S *T*REATISE STOP *H*AVE *E*VER-HARD *G*OING *A*FTER *M*Y *E*NCYCLOPDIA

and it was signed—*FLOWER.*

DEATH'S TOY SHOP

JANE WEST pecked falteringly at her typewriter. She peered near-sightedly at the shorthand notebook on the desk beside her, twisted ill-shod feet under her chair, stopped to erase what she had written, began again. Her dress of cheap rayon hung clumsily from stooped shoulders to lump in awkward folds about her more awkward form. Her hair, if washed, might have shown tawny lights, but it was grotesquely frizzed in a pitiful attempt at coquetry and her mouth gaped half-open, giving to her carbon-smudged face an expression of fairly blatant stupidity.

The man in the doorway of the office that was partitioned off from the big loft watched her with contempt in his shadowed gaze. But there was satisfaction, too. This was what one would expect, he seemed to be thinking, when one hired a seven-dollar-a-week stenographer from a fly-by-night business school. And it was exactly what he wanted.

Beyond the railed-off enclosure in which Jane worked, cluttered shelving went row upon row back into obscurity. The objects filling those shelves were weird and wonderful. Here a collection of tin frogs squatted, vividly green, waiting for someone to wind their springs and give them life. Next to them a horde of miniature hula dancers, shameless in short net skirts and nothing else, poised rivet-jointed limbs in expectancy of the same magical touch.

There were woolly prize-fighters, black and white. There were polka-dotted beetles big as a baby's fist, lifelike flies heading carded stickpins; an infinite variety of puzzles and games; miniature playing cards with which no game could be played because no single suit was complete. Gargoylesque masks hung in clusters from the drab ceiling. This was the stock, in short, of a "pitchman's" supply house, destined to be hawked on street corners and at county fairs, or to serve as prizes at boardwalk and pleasure park concessions.

The Arnerico-Oriental Trading Company dealt in gim-crackery and brummagem. And in death!

If the loft's one huge window had not been almost opaque with encrusted dirt, Jane West might have looked out through it over a pinnacled city in whose canyons six million people went about their early evening pursuits in fancied security. She might have seen the lights of an airplane that was burring westward to carry its mail and its passengers over three thousand miles of smiling, peaceful countryside; over a hundred million Americans unaware that the shadow of mass murder hovered over them; of sudden, unpresaged disaster; of rapine and arson and merciless, terrible slaughter. But Jane picked out a few words, wrinkled her freckled nose in dismay, reached for her eraser....

"I want that letter to get out tonight," her employer said, in the precise, unaccented syllables of the educated alien. "You've been at it an hour now."

THE GIRL looked up, tears in her gray eyes. "But Mr.

Carron," she wailed. "You're always so petickler 'bout every word bein' spelled jest right, an' about all them dozens an' grosses in the orders. You'll yell if I make a mistake. An' you make me nervous, standin' there an' watchin' me like that. As if—as if you t'ought I might steal somethin' or somethin'.'"

Carron's thin lips twitched with covert amusement. "I was not watching you, Jane," he responded. "I am expecting a very good customer from Mexico, and he's late." He was short, spare in his dark suit. His patent-leather shoes were pointed, almost effeminately small. The faintest of blues tinged the crescents of his carefully tended fingernails. His cheekbones were slightly too high, his black eyes vaguely almond-shaped. "I was wondering if anything—if he has been delayed. No, young lady, I trust you implicitly...."

"Thank you, Mr. Carron."

"I'm right in trusting you, aren't I, Jane?" The man's voice dropped a note, slurred. "You wouldn't by any chance talk to anyone about my business?" It was a low purr, somehow menacing, somehow infinitely cruel. "You wouldn't try to listen at my keyhole?"

The cloddish girl looked bewildered, surprised in a dull sort of way. "Law, Mr. Carron! What would anyone be asking about your business for? An' how could I listen at the keyhole when I'm all the time busy writing. It's all I kin do to get my work out, let alone monkeyin' aroun' with what ain't none of my affairs."

An icy smile licked Carron's sallow countenance. "No," he murmured, half to himself. "There isn't room in that dull brain

of yours for even feminine curiosity.—Oh, hello, Señor Gonzales. Come in! Come right in."

The elevator door had slid open, and a tall, cadaverously thin individual had stepped out of it. His pointed fingers twirled the end of a pointed black mustache; his chin, his nose, were pointed; his eyes were black, glittering points in a swarthy, hollow-checked face. He clicked his heels, bowed, and one listened for the jingle of spurs and the rattle of a sword.

"Señor Carron!" he exclaimed. "I am desolate' zat I am late. Bot your so-beeg ceety, eet ees meex me all up."

"Pretty puzzling for a stranger," Carron smiled. "But you got here all right. Come on inside and we'll get right down to business. I've got the greatest set-up you ever heard of for your *fiesta.* "

Gonzales' heels *tack-tacked* on the unwashed wooden floor, and Jane's typewriter took up its halting *tack-tack* again. The two men vanished inside Carron's private office. The door closed behind them.

The sound of its closing was metallic. Strange, that in this shabby establishment the ceiling-high partition in which that door was set should be of heavy steel.

Stranger still was the change that came over Jane West. She was suddenly tense, vibrant with incongruous excitement. And while one hand still peeked at the typewriter, she did a very queer thing. She bent. The fingers of her free hand fumbled within the side of one of her disreputable shoes. They fished out two threadlike wires, jabbed their stripped ends into the slits on each side of a floor board far under the desk. Then Jane straightened, and once more was laboring, nearsightedly, falteringly, at her typewriter. Its *tack-tack* spat against the steel partition, penetrated it, assuring the men behind it that she was still at her desk, so far from them that what they said could not possibly be overheard.

BUT JANE WEST'S head was canted to one side, pressing one ear against a raised shoulder, against a flat disk that was hidden by the sleazy fabric covering that shoulder. And the voices of Messrs. Gonzales and Carron whispered very clearly in that ear.

"What happened?" Carron snapped. "Why are you late?"

"I was followed all ze way from Agualeguas. On ze train I could not get reed of my shadow, bot wiz a leetle ingeenuity, in ze ceety, he was—pouf."

"You are sure you got rid of him?"

"I am Señor Alcido Tiano!" Insulted pride was in the reply. "I would not be alife eef long ago I deed not learn how to deal wiz spies."

"Good Lord! What...?"

"A man lies in an alley, far from here, wiz a knife slash across ze gullet. *Finee.*"

"I wish that had not happened." The man called Carron sounded worried. "It would be too bad if at the last minute you were traced here. This set-up is perfeet. It has been quite natural for this kind of business to be sending and receiving letters from all over the country, and with all the items it handles easy to work out an unsuspectable code. And since most of the goods I handle are made in the Far East, neither my cables nor my letters to—our employers—have been subject to suspicion. If the police should trace you here now...."

"Zey deed not trace me." Gonzales—or Tiano—seemed very sure of himself. "An' it weel make no deeference aftair tonight."

"After—You mean...?"

"I mean zat eef you haf done your part properlee, zere will no longer be any necessitee for secrecy aftair ze clock strikes

146

seven. Our forces are massed along ze bordair, from ze Gulf of Mexeeco to ze Gulf of California. Ze fleet of—our allies—ees in ze Paceefic, wiz thousands of ze bombeeng planes ready to take off for ze attack. Remains only your word zat you are readee. Eef you geev me eet, zere weel be a telephone call here from Tito Manuon een an hour from now. He ees schedule to play ze guitar from ze WROW on a national—how you call?—hook 'em up. Eef I geeve him ze wor' to play ze...."

"*Mañana Rumba.* I know. That's the signal for everything to start. God, man, haven't I been thinking about it, dreaming about it, for months? Well, you can tell him to play it. My men are ready. Trained, armed with the machine-guns and grenades and gas-bombs I've been sending, bit by bit, in my shipments. They'll strike at the signal, invade every State Capital, every city hall of any importance and take a thousand hostages. The President is speaking tonight at a political rally. We'll either capture him or kill him. The country will be paralyzed, disorganized. We'll make our own terms by noon tomorrow, and they'll be harsh ones."

"Good. Vary good. My congratulations, Señor Ho Chien. We will show ze worl' how to make war."

"Thanks, Tiano. Well, since we've got nothing more to do till Manuon calls, suppose we have a drink."

JANE WEST was white, gasping. She had suspected the cables and letters to be coded, but since the cipher was an arbitrary one had not been able to get the details of the conspiracy. She had waited, discovery, death, always at her elbows, for this moment of illumination. She must get out of here....

"Zere *ees* somesing more, my fran'. *Zat girl, outside....*"

147

Jane pushed shaking hands down the desktop, shoving herself up from her chair. But her foot held the dictaphone connection, momentarily.

"Hell! She's all right. She's so stupid she doesn't know her knee from her elbow. I'll tell her—"

"She may be stupeed, bot I trus' no one. Get her een here. We shall keep her here teel eet ees too late for her to betray us."

"All right, Tiano, if you—"

Jane was on her feet. She threw a despairing glance to the emergency stairway door. It was locked, barred. No time…. She darted to the elevator, thumbed both down and up buttons. If only the car were right here…!

"Jane!" Carron's—Ho Chien's—silken voice sounded behind her. "Where are you going?"

She turned. "I was just goin' to run aroun' the corner to let my boy friend know I was goin' to be late. I got a supper date wit' him."

"Yes?" The man's eyes narrowed. "Well, I need you here. You can telephone him."

"He ain't got no 'phone. An' he's that jealous he'll be coming here to see what's the matter if I don't let him know I'm all right."

She had no real hope that she could get away. But she had to try something, anything. Tiano pushed past Carron. There was a gun in his hand.

"You weel go nowhere, mees," he snapped. "You weel—" Red light flickered over her head. The elevator was about to stop. "Wan wor' to ze boy an' you both die."

The lift door slid open. "Down," the black-faced operator called. "Who's gwine down?"

"No wan. Bot eef you weel wait just a leetle meen-ute—" Tiano's gun was concealed under his coat, but Jane knew it was there, agonizingly knew that a single word from her would being lethal lead flaming into her body, into the Negro's—"Mees—zis young lady would lak you to deleever a note for her. She weel write eet now." And their deaths would accomplish nothing. "To someone she likes so mooch she would like to see heem again, some day."

His meaning was plain. He was offering her life in exchange for lulling the suspicions of a possible confederate.

"Yes, Jimmy," Jane's lips could hardly form the words. "That's what I wanted."

"Zere ees a quarter for you eef you weel take ze message."

"Sure, mister," the boy grinned. "I got time now. Everybody else is gone. I'm just waitin' fer you folks to close up."

"Zat ees good. All right, Mees. Write w'at you want to say."

Jane dragged herself to her desk, her limbs moving as though through some viscid, invisible fluid. She stuck a sheet of the Americo-Oriental's stationery in the machine, wrote:

PAT DEAR:
The boss has a lot of work for me and I can't get away. I'll see you in the morning, if I can, to hear how the game comes out. Be careful, dear. You never played for such high stakes before.

You understand, don't you?

FLOWER

149

She was conscious that Tiano was reading over her shoulder. "I was going to watch him play bridge," she said, "for a lot of money." She folded the paper, addressed the envelope. "Mr. Ford Duane,—Fourth Avenue."

"Pat?" the Mexican arched his eyebrows. "Flower?"

"They're our pet names for each other," the girl explained. "We always use them." She licked the envelope closed, started back to the elevator. "Here, Jimmy—"

"No! Wait!" Tiano intercepted her, took the envelope from her. "I haf just theenk, I mus' go out myself. I weel deleever ze note."

The elevator door clanged shut. Jane stared at it, gelid fingers squeezing her throat. Tiano had tricked her. He had guessed that the note might conceal a warning, and was making sure that there would be no interference with his plans. "I know how to deal wiz spies," he had said. "A knife slash across ze gullet...."

"Come on inside here," Ho Chien purred. "We'll wait for Tiano to get back." His tongue licked his lips. "He's an artist with that knife of his. Between the two of us I think we're going to have some very interesting entertainment while we're waiting for Manuon's call."

FORD DUANE, alpaca-coated, lank, stooped under a lassitude too dreary for his apparent youth, sat at a shabby desk near the front of his second-hand bookstore. A pencil in his long, slim fingers idly traced a rose on the dust-filmed desk-blotter, and he seemed half-asleep.

The shadows were thick and dark between the towering tiers of tattered books that filled the dusty store. Outside, wan streetlamps struggled vainly against the night, filling the grimy Fourth Avenue block that is known as the Port of Missing Books. In all the peaceful land, there could be no spot more somnolently peaceful than this.

And yet death was a living, breathing presence in this sleepy store. Duane's ears were attuned to every footfall, every slither of movement, in the street outside. The keen blue eyes under his drooped lids slid, every now and then, to peer through an artfully contrived aperture in the piled books of his window-display. Eternal vigilance was the price Ford Duane paid for life itself!

He was not, by far, the defeated dealer in discarded volumes that he seemed.

All over the world a secret, deadly Game is being played, a game the stakes of which are nations themselves. Spy and counter-spy, saboteur and masked guard, the players of the Game fight an endless war. Unknown to the people they attack and protect, unknown even to each other, they breathe danger every second of the day, the year. They fight, and die, unwept. No medals are pinned on their breasts, no wreaths are laid on their tombs.

The rules of the Game are rigid. They say that the players must remain nameless, unknown to one another, team-mates as well as antagonists. But Nature scoffs at man-made rules. Ford Duane was a champion in the Game. But for months a face had hovered in his thoughts. A sweet mouth, formed for kissing. Gray, brooding eyes. Tawny hair in which light glinted duskily.

He knew her only as "Flower." Drawing the rose on the desk, he wondered where she was. Whether she was still alive. She might lie in a nameless grave, for all he knew, and his heart with her.

But he did not forget to watch the street through the aperture in the window. He did not forget that his identity and his lair might somehow have been discovered. There was a price on his head in the chancelleries of half the world. There were those who needed no price to make them thirst for his blood. Now, even now, death might be stalking him.

A footfall thudded on the sidewalk. A tall, cadaverous man came into view. He had a white envelope in his hand, and every once in a while he would look up at the numbers on the store doors, scrutinizing them. Ford Duane watched him.

The man reached the front of Duane's bookstore. His waxed mustache twitched. He turned. He was coming in.

The glass-panelled door opened, closed again. "Señor Ford Duane?" Alcido Tiano inquired, bowing.

"I am Duane," Ford rose. "What can I do for you, sir?"

"Sometimes known as 'Pat?'"

"Yes." There was no surprise in Duane's reply, no change in his expression. But a pulse throbbed in his wrists. Pat! The three letters, P-A-T, were a signal to him that he was again being called to sit in on the Game. In many and various ways that signal had reached him, and always after that men had died. Perhaps, this time, it would be his turn to die. "Yes. I am called that by one or two close friends."

"Ah. Zen zis lettair ees for you." The Mexican slid it onto the desk. "Perhaps zere ees an answair. Eef you don't mind I weel look at your so manee books." He was infinitely suave, infinitely courteous. "I haf ze passion for ol' books."

"Of course." Duane watched Tiano move away, far back into the shelf-cast shadows, heels clicking on the floor. Then he picked up the envelope, opened it.

"Pat dear: The boss—You understand, don't you? Flower!" LITTLE MUSCLES ridged Duane's blunt jaw. Her hand had written this note! But what did it mean? There was no indication of what code she had used. It was too short for any code....

"Zis first edeetion of Butler's Hudibras!" the messenger's excited exclamation came from the gloomy depths of the store. "Weel you come here please, Señor Duane? I weesh to ask you...."

Of course! The real message was verbal. Flower's note was only an introduction, a warning that the bearer was to be trusted. The man wanted Duane to come away from the front of the store, to where there would be no possibility of their colloquy being observed by some chance entrant.

"Right with you, sir." Duane thrust the letter into the breast pocket of his alpaca coat, where it rustled against the dried petals of a rose whose faint fragrance had reminded him for weeks that once it had been a token from the Flower that she had escaped a lethal trap. He padded back between the high bookstacks, rounded the end of one of them to whence Tiano's voice had sounded.

He wasn't there. No one.... A shadow moved on the floor...! Duane whirled, his muscles exploding into instantaneous

153

action. A lithe figure leaped at him from the covert to which it had moved, knife-metal glinting in a down-flailing arc. Duane ducked, lightning-swift, under the murder-blade. The outflick of his fists was a rapier thrust, pounding one-two into the assassin's belly. Then his fingers, steel strong, were clenched on Tiano's knife-wrist and his free hand was darting under the lapel of his gray jacket.

"Sacre!" the Mexican hissed. "You are too smart." His features contorted, a gargoyle-writhing mask of malevolence. "Bot how do you like—thees." His other hand lashed out, stabbing another knife at Duane's breast. So close he was that it could not miss....

A jet of thin vapor spewed from under Ford's coat, into Tiano's face. And the killer was suddenly nerveless, limp—the knife clattering from his fingers, his thin body slumping after it—collapsing like a gutted meal sack.

Ford Duane stood above his victim, swaying. Once again unremitting watchfulness, split-second coördination of senses and brain and muscles, utter preparedness for any eventuality, had saved him. But he knew the adventure was not ended. It had only begun. There was no doubt that the Flower had written that note. The signature itself was known only to the two of them. The very fact that the killer had brought it told him that she was in dire danger.

Or that she was beyond all help.

The American's countenance was a grim false face, his eyes two glowing, terrible orbs. Her message was concealed in the apparently meaningless words, then. What was it? He did not have to take it out of his pocket. Every character was burned into his brain.

"... I can't get away." She was a prisoner, somewhere. Possibly in the office on whose letterhead the letter was typed—"the boss" indicated that. "I'll see you—if I can." She knew herself to be in deadly peril. "... How the game comes out." "The game"— there was only one Game to the two of them, the game they played against death and the secret armies of their country's secret enemies. "... You never played for such high stakes...."

Such—high—stakes. The stakes of their Game were always the safety of America. *If he had never before played for such high stakes....*

He must find her—at once. Time later to decide what to do about the assassin he had vanquished. Duane dropped to one knee. There was strong cord in his pocket. Lashed about the man's wrists, his ankles, it should keep him safe....

A DESK-CLOCK ticked loudly in the stillness. The girl who called herself Jane West sat slumped in a chair, her wide, staring eyes fixed on the dial of that clock, and on the telephone next to it. Ho Chien sat bolt upright in another chair, a window behind him framing his exotic figure, his peculiarly round head. His hands played idly with a pearl-handled revolver on the desk-top, but his blue-nailed forefinger was never far from its trigger.

Jane knew that the instant she tried to move out of her chair a bullet would thud into her quivering flesh.

"You were very clever, my girl." Ho Chien said chattily. "I never would have thought of looking into the box you had standing against the partition, where you kept that hat of yours so it wouldn't get dusty. Smart to have the microphone and amplifier in its false bottom, picking up the vibration of voices from in here. But it's all over now."

No use for deception any longer. "Maybe it isn't all over yet," Jane said quietly.

"Your friend Tiano hasn't returned, and it is three minutes to seven already."

The man smiled, without humor. "That will not make any difference. If Tiano is not back when Manuon calls, I will tell him to play the *Mañana Rumba*. And after that—you will pay for deceiving me—as many other of your female compatriots will pay, tomorrow and tomorrow and tomorrow."

There was terrible significance in the way his lips curled back from his pointed teeth. It told Jane what lay in store for the women of her country if ever that lilting melody was broadcast. The pulsing strains to which they had so often danced would be a signal of despair for them.

The clock ticked, ticked, each separate tick a hammer blow of agony on her soul. Duane had not received her note. No— Tiano had taken it to him—and had killed him. That was why the Mexican was not back. He had been caught, arrested. But the dreadful deed was done. Otherwise Duane would be here....

Tick. Tick. Tick. Two minutes more. Oh God! Two minutes to seven. Two minutes to—*Hell.*

Tiano wasn't back yet. Maybe Ho Chien was lying. Maybe Manuon would not take orders from him.

"I arranged for Tito Manuon's time on the broadcast," the

spymaster answered her unspoken thought. "He will do whatever I say."

No hope. No hope anywhere. The fate of a nation, of America, trembled in the balance. And there was nothing she could do. Nothing anyone could do, now.

Jane West could not know it, but five stories below a frantic man rattled the knob of a door that was closed and locked, a man who had been led to the address by the letterhead on Jane's note. Inside that door a Negro boy and a grizzled watchman lay on the lobby floor, their throats slit from ear to ear. Alcido Tiano did not believe in taking any chances....

Tick. Tick. Tick. The longer hand of the desk clock moved, imperceptibly, indomitably, toward the end of the hour. To the end of America's last hour of freedom. In cactus thickets swarthy men crouched, muffling the clank of their rifles, nursing their machine guns. Far out on the Pacific great gray vessels rose and fell on a heaving tide, and stocky, saffron-visaged pilots warmed up the motors of great bombing planes. In a thousand cellars in a thousand cities, other men waited, waited—for seven o'clock and the palpitant, throbbing strains of the *Mañana Rumba*....

AND IN a fifth floor New York office—the only lighted office in the building—a tawny-haired girl watched a clock's minute hand move, her dilated eyes measuring the distance between herself and the telephone that stood next to the clock. If she moved swiftly enough, she wondered, when the telephone bell started to ring, would her momentum carry her across that space, as bullets pounded into her? Would there be life enough left in her when she got across it to smash the instrument to the floor, to smash it so that it could not be used? Even if she did, would Manuon give the signal anyway?

Tick. She could only try. *Tick.* It was the only chance left and if it did not come off she would be dead anyway. Tick. She would want to be dead. Tick. Thirty seconds more. Her muscles gathered for the desperate effort, her eyes clouding to veil her intention. *Tick....*

Glass smashed in, from the window! A swirl of black draperies showed in the jagged aperture for an instant. Ho Chien twisted....

An appalling figure leaped into the room from the fire escape, led to the room by the lighted window. Tall, black-swathed, black-masked. Felt hat pulled low down. Black-gloved hand outthrust, a curiously thick-barreled pistol snouting from it. The finger curled about that trigger startlingly, awesomely red; the red of spurting blood.

It was the sight of that finger that paralyzed Ho Chien for an all-important instant. Long enough for Jane to leap from her chair and knock the pearl-handled revolver out of his reach. Then a name spewed from his suddenly pallid lips.

"Red Finger!"

A word of terror, that name, in the subterranean world where the endless war is fought. Ace of counter-spies, the bravest of America's secret enemies trembled at the very thought of Red Finger. Many had died at his hands, many had limped home to tell of failure at the moment of success. But he wore no medals. He was on no Roll of Honor... and never would be!

"Yes, I am Red Finger. Your hands up, Ho Chien. Way up...."

Jane didn't hear the rest. She heard only the shrill clamor of the telephone. She twisted, reaching for the cradled instrument....

A shot barked. A red hot slug pounded into her shoulder, slammed her across the desk.

"I weel take zat call," a voice said, and there were shots again, loud and thunderous in the small room. Tiano was flinging into it, his gun spewing orange-red flame at Red Finger, at Jane. Ho Chien was on the floor, wet, pungent mist from the thick-barrelled pistol following him down, but the American counter-spy was disarmed, his curious weapon shot from his hand. He was darting about the room, dodging Tiano's flaming bullets. The telephone clamored. Lethal lead plucked at Red Finger's black cloak.

The Mexican reached the desk, reached for the receiver. Jane, rolling in her agony, sank sharp, fierce teeth in his wrist. He cursed, struck at her with his gun-barrel. The sight slashed her cheek.

Red Finger leaped, a great black bat swooping through midair, spattering blood-drops as it flew. He came down on Tiano's shoulders. The two pounded to the floor. Jane plucked the telephone receiver from its cradle.

"Hello." There was none of her pain, her agony, in her voice. "Hello, Manuon."

"Who ees zis?" the receiver squeaked in her ear. "I want to talk to...."

"Señor Tiano? He is unable to answer you, Señor Manuon. He is very busy. But he wants me to tell you not to play the

Mañana Rumba. Something has happened at the last moment to change his plans."

The hard rubber cylinder slipped from her strengthless fingers. Dizzying dark pulsed about her....

Red Finger pushed himself up from the floor. His black cloak was clotted, viscid, gashed in countless places. He swayed, looking down at the writhing figure at his feet.

"I thought," he choked, "I left you safely tied up."

A snarling smile twisted Alcido Tiano's face. "You forget eet ees Tiano wiz whom you deal. Zere ees no rope made zat weel hol' ze great Tiano. Especially eef eet ees in a place where zere are sharp edges on all ze feet of ze book shelves, place' zere by a man who expec's sometime to be tied up in hees own store."

"I would have remembered that," Red Finger's voice sounded as if he was laughing, with pain threading his laughter, "if I hadn't been thinking about a flower." He stopped. There was no use talking to a dead man, a man whose spine had been snapped by a trick of *jiu-jitsu* learned long ago.

MANY MESSAGES throbbed out over the Americo-Oriental's telephone that night. There were thousands of quiet arrests, all over the country, thousands of prisoners in Federal jails the next morning. A gray fleet steamed home, baffled. Disappointed bands of marauders skulked across cactus prickled deserts, cached their weapons against a revolution that sooner or later would be sure to come....

But before those messages started, before Jane West got out her lists of addresses and her files of letters, there was a very human moment in the dusty fifth floor office where one man lay dead and another unconscious. A moment in which soft words were whispered that had nothing to do with the Game. A moment in which lips met in a caress older, by many centuries, than the endless war.

ENVOY OF DOOM

FORD DUANE, tall and lank and wearily stooped, slowly threaded a shadowy labyrinth of tall bookstacks. Outside, the hush of dusk, gray with quiet melancholy, brooded between the drab facades of the ancient loft buildings that line the Fourth Avenue block so completely given over to the sale of dog-eared, tattered volumes it is known as the Port of Missing Books.

Elsewhere New York was astir with the bustle of home-seeking thousands, was alive with the roar of traffic, the chatter of many voices, the tramp of many footfalls. Here the wide-flung turmoil was muted to a dull, rumbling growl that disturbed not at all the street's dusty drowse.

Here the threat of Death brooded. Within this somnolent shop peril lurked tigress-like; a gray, indomitable shadow waiting for the inevitable instant when momentarily its quarry's guard must relax. It would leap then, a gray flash, and strike steel claws into Ford Duane's flesh, sink tearing fangs into his throat.

Duane came to the pamphlet-hung door of the store, reached a slow hand to the switch that would light the single cluttered display window. The street lamps blinked on, abruptly necklacing the quiet block with high-hung, bright topazes....

A lilting whistle sprayed the hush with the first notes of

'Pennies from Heaven.' Shuffling footfalls were startingly loud, coming along the sidewalk.

Duane's fingers hesitated for an eyeblink of time, then clicked over the switch tumbler. The dingy luminance from his window streamed across the pavement. The bookseller had tensed, almost imperceptibly.

His lids drooped a bit more, as if the better to hide the sudden keen stab of blue eyes beneath them. A shadow blotted the cracked concrete and then the whistler came into the frame of the doorway.

He was a boy, a gamin of the gutters shabbily clothed, his freckles almost hidden by grime, his hatless hair unkempt and startlingly red. Duane knew at once, though he seemed not to see him at all, that the youngster's shoes were broken, that his frayed knickers had been clumsily patched at the knees, and that there was a rather awkwardly wrapped small package in one dirty hand.

The alpaca-smocked shopkeeper relaxed. Nothing to worry about.... The boy turned and slouched toward him past a trestled box with the sign YOUR CHOICE-15¢ 2 for 25.

"Dis Duane's bookstore?" he asked. "Yuh Mr. Duane?"

"Yes, son."

"A guy over on Toid Av'noo gimme dis package ter bring yuh." The lad made no move to hand it to Duane. "He said he found it w'ere he woiks in de Brighton cafeteria and yuh must uh lost it dere when yuh came in for a cup uh coffee this afternoon. He said ter say Pat found it and decided he'd better send it."

"Pat? Oh, yes. The bus-boy!" Duane had not left his store

163

that day. He knew no one in the Brighton Cafeteria named Pat. "I'll have to give him a tip next time I see him." But the letters composing that name—P-A-T—had a startling meaning to him. "And here's a quarter for you." As the initials of the title of a book offered for sale, as the first letters of a peddler's cry, in many other forms, they had presaged the delivery of a message to Ford Duane, had each time presaged a bout with danger, with death.

Hitherto it had been the death of others those letters had prefaced. This time it might mean his own.

He fished in his pocket, exchanged a worn silver disk for the string-tied bundle. "T'anks, mister," the youngster grunted, and darted away, his whistle jubilant.

DUANE DID not move from the doorway. His veiled look furtively probed the deepening twilight. Across the street, in an unlighted vestibule between two shops differing from his only by the scabrously lettered names on the unwashed glass of their windows, a man dawdled.

Holding the package, Duane went out and straightened the contents of his sidewalk boxes. He was clearly visible in the light from his store, in the illumination of the nearest street lamp. He tore the paper from the bundle, crumpled it and tossed it into the gutter. He shook out the folded fabric about which it had been wrapped.

The thing was a worn and shabby silk scarf of a nondescript gray that exactly matched the drabness of his appearance. Fumbling absent-mindedly, he adjusted a cardboard sign; NATIONAL GEOGRAPHICS 10¢; and wandered slowly back into his store.

Set back from the entrance, but still exposed to the view of the lounger, there was a flat-top desk. Duane switched on a goose-necked lamp so that its light fell brightly on the desk's cluttered surface, negligently tossed down the scarf. As if by accident the silk band spread itself as it fell, so that it lay smoothly over a pile of dog-eared catalogues, under the lamp.

Ford Duane let himself down into a creaking swivel chair before the desk, picked up a book that had been lying face down and open, among the chaos of dusty papers. He took a spectacle case from the pocket of his smock, adjusted them to his eyes and settled back to read.

If the lounger across the street had been able to peer through Duane's glasses, he would not have seen the page of the volume the bookseller was apparently perusing, but the hem of the scarf he seemed to have forgotten—startlingly magnified. He would have seen the stitches binding the silken hem stand out like heavy twine against he gray background, and he would have seen that those stitches were by no means of the same length.

There were long stitches and short ones, four close rows of them, and there did not seem to be any pattern to them, nor any reason for the variation save that the hem had been sewn by hand rather than machine. But Ford Duane read them as dots and dashes forming letters in the Continental Morse code; forming words....

"Warehouse rear of three six three Ave E investigate and spot leaders but take no action"

The glint of excitement in Duane's hidden orbs died away as he read the three last words of that message. He would chafe,

he knew, at the leash they place upon him. But he was a soldier, and he must obey orders.

He was a uniformed soldier in the invisible army that unceasingly, unendingly fights a hidden war against hidden enemies. Victory means for the men—and the women—of that army no medals, no plaudits, no parades before a grateful, cheering nation. Defeat means for them—death. A lonely death at the hands of their country's furtive enemies, and an anonymous grave.

They are the great gray army of peace. Unnamed, unhonored, they battle eternally against a host of silent, gray invaders who gnaw constantly at the foundations of our commonwealth, preparing in time of peace for the war their masters hope sometime to force upon us, when we have been weakened enough.

Duane's head nodded over his book, as though it had sent him to sleep. The man in the vestibule across the street strolled away. After awhile Ford Duane roused himself to take in the sidewalk boxes; to lock his door, and turn out the light in the window.

He wandered back to the rear of the store, where a half-open curtain marked off but did not conceal the narrow alcove that a rumpled camp cot and a two-burner gas plate atop an upended box marked as his living quarters. He turned on a light there, made his frugal meal, ate it. Then he rose, pulled the curtain together.

Behind the cot there was a frosted window. If anyone were watching that window, he would have seen Duane's shadow move back and forth, undressing. He would have seen the silhouetted form of the bookseller lie down on the cot at last, a book propped up on his chest. He would have waited long, and after awhile gotten tired of waiting, to see that shadow move again.

A flitting smile relieved the gravity of Ford Duane's countenance as he glanced up from the floor at the dummy he had arranged on the camp cot. He crawled along the floor till he had reached a certain spot to one side of the cubicle. He pressed on a certain board, on another.

There was the rasp of wood on wood. There was, quite suddenly, a square black hole in the floor. The swift slither of a lithe body, the rasp of wood on wood once more, and the hole was gone. There was no form any longer in the back room of Ford Duane's Secondhand Bookshop, except the unmoving, dummy figure on the bed.

IN A dark, waterfront alley that should he deserted at night, a tall, lank shadow moved briefly. It merged with the impenetrable black along the wooden wall of a one-story shack that leaned wearily against the high dark loom of a warehouse whose few windows were sightless eyes in its streaked brick facade.

Sounds came into that alley. The swish of roiled river water close by. The chug, chug of some motorboat prowling the darkness, and the far-off, melancholy hoot of some ferryboat nearing its wharf.

Nearer, within the alley itself there was another sound.

Dull, wall-muffled, it was a rhythmic thud, thud, thud. It was a single repeated sound like the pound of a huge machine and yet it was somehow too widely dispersed to be made by a single object. It seemed to come from behind the full width of the warehouse wall. It was now louder, now almost inaudible, as though that which caused it approached the brick cliff, receded from it, approached it again.

There was somehow something ominous about that sound.

The rotted roof boards of the wooden lean-to creaked whisperingly. The shadow that had been in the alley drifted across it. A chink of light showed in the warehouse wall.

The rhythmic sound cut short. The shadow crouched against the rust-frayed iron shutter through which filtered that yellow light-thread. It was man-form, but it had no face.

Within the warehouse, partitions had been ripped out, making one huge room. The glare of two five-hundred watt lamps hung from the high ceiling filled the enormous chamber.

Beneath them a long double-line of men in vivid green shirts stood stiffly, heels together, stomachs in, chests out.

The lines were ruler straight, as was the serried hedge of sticks, like unpainted canes without ferrules or handles, slanted across the men's shoulders. Each individual had a white arm-band just above the bend of his elbow, and each arm band was marked in black with the insignia of a certain world-power whose leader only the day before had orated fulsomely concerning the friendship between his country and America.

A hulking, square-shouldered, square-featured man faced the motionless ranks. His hair was a white, stiff pompadour bristling the flat top of his skull. His eyes were small, piglike, below a beetling, corrugated brow. His shirt was also green, but the arm-band on its sleeve was black, the insignia white.

Black Band's square jaw was thrust out. His gross lips barked a command.

Two rows of left legs slanted up and out, stiff-kneed, jerked down. Right legs came up in perfect unison, jerked down. Two lines of manikins moved forward—*thud*, thud,—*one*, two, *one*, two—*thud*, thud, *thud*, thud.

The lines thudded across the bare, splintered floor as if long, rigid rods ran through the men's waists, their heels. They weren't men. They were machines. They were one machine, everything human blasted out of them.

Thud, thud. *Thud*, thud. Black Band snapped an order. The company front broke into fours, was a column of fours—*thud*, thud, *thud*, thud—right-angled along a corner, angled again, formed twos. Black Band drove them, wove intricate patterns

169

of them all over the expanse of gray, clean-swept wood—*thud,* thud, *thud,* thud. The legs flashed up and down again, piston-like up and down. The bodies moved like cogs on a conveyor belt, like a machine. The heels hammered on the floor, pounded on the wood, hammered out hate; hammered out war; shaped death; forged destruction. *Thud,* thud. *One,* two. *One,* two. *Thud,* thud, *thud....*

Black Band barked, and the lines were immobile once more, frozen. Black Band wheeled sharply, clicked heels together, was a ramrod stiff, rigid statue. His right arm angled to his forehead, its fingers stiffly horizontal.

Narrow, ladderlike stairs pitched sharply down from a square opening in the ceiling. A short slender man stood halfway down the stairs; round thick lenses making owl-like his sharp, rapacious features. His pinch-nostrilled nose was a hooked beak. The tiny black dab of a mustache under it only accentuated the sexless cruelty of his colorless lips.

The newcomer went up again through the ceiling. Black Band wheeled, barked. The lines broke. The machines were men again; shabby except for the green shirts from whose sleeves they tore the arm bands as they poured across the loft toward where clothing was piled in a long heap against the wall. Black Band strode to the stairs, climbed out of sight.

The men were overcoated, hatted, and they looked like two-score young men who had been attending a meeting of some social club that now was breaking up. They seemed in no hurry to leave, but the group steadily dwindled.

IN THE alley there was the sound of a cautiously opened door, the sound of cautious feet slinking toward the river. After a space during which one might count ten the same sounds once more disturbed the murky silence.

When the great loft had been thus entirely drained of its occupants, the lights blinked out. The room was absolutely dark, absolutely lifeless.

Just over the threshold of hearing, metal clicked against metal. Rusted hinges rasped briefly. There was a whisper of movement in the blackness. A stair tread creaked, as though the warehouse's old timbers were settling a bit.

There was no longer any shadow on the lean-to roof.

On the floor above that where a secret company had drilled, the darkness was just as intense, but here there was a low murmur of voices from somewhere far back, and a sense that the space was filled to its ceiling by huge black hulks.

Jute-covered bales were piled there, through whose burlap a probing hand might manage to feel round hard objects; the size of coconuts and as round.

They were not coconuts. They were too regularly corrugated for that, and the chill of metal penetrated through the jute. They were bombs in those mounded bales, thousands of hand grenades that needed only the release of a tiny lever to blast all about them into fragments. Beyond them were high stacks of flat cases, just the length of rifles, and beyond those, other, stubbier cases that might quite possibly contain ammunition for those rifles.

At the rear of this storage room with its curious contents, a small space was partitioned off by a solid board wall that reached to the ceiling. Within the windowless chamber thus formed was a table on which a large and detailed map of the United States was outspread, a map studded by pins with varicolored heads, by tiny, multihued flags.

A great slate slab was bracketed to the room's rear wall, its surface gleaming with copper bus-bars, with bright switches, with the white-faced dials of gauges. Black wires coiled from the slab to another, smaller table whose surface was entirely covered by the orderly tangle of a radio telephone receiver and transmitter.

A wizened, pasty-faced little man crouched over this table, perched tensely at the very edge of a chair, the round black disks of ear-phones clamped to his head. There were chairs near the larger table, but the three men clustered around it were on their feet, and they were bent over the map for all the world like the General Staff of an army in the midst of a long battle, planning the next day's strategy.

"Reports from the West Coast," Owl-Eyes said, "are very satisfactory." His voice was sexless as his mouth. "Friday the longshoremen will again go on strike. The seamen will join them."

"That will go well enough now without more help from us." Black Band spoke with thick-tongued, guttural satisfaction. "They are stubborn, those brutes who load and unload the vessels and those who handle them, and the ship-owners are just as stubborn. There will be trouble. This time, with the arms and bombs with which the strikers have been supplied from a mysterious source about which they have not asked many questions, that trouble will not be over till America no longer has a merchant fleet on the Pacific."

"In the coal mines," Owl-Eyes' white, slim hand gestured across the map's east central portion, "they have been sitting down for a week, but the governors of Pennsylvania and West Virginia have almost brought the union and the owners together."

"Tonight that is true," Black Band agreed, "but here," his spatulate thumb pressed down a pin in Pennsylvania's Carbon County, "at dawn tomorrow, a company guard will be shot at from the entrance of mine. He will not be injured, because he is one of ours, but he will fire back, and before what that commences is ended the flame of riot will be a conflagration and there will be no hope of peace between miners and operators."

"We have enough trained men on both sides to make certain of that," Owl Eyes explained.

Both men, their perfect English only slightly marred by a vaguely foreign intonation, were quite evidently speaking for the benefit of the third.

HE WAS shorter than either, and so grossly obese that his torso was a flabby sphere. His hair was thin on his glistening scalp and the great billows of fat that formed his cheeks and his grotesquely narrow neck swamped his queerly tiny features, so that only his shrewd little eyes seemed alive. His columnar arms ended in hands that were crudely shaped blobs the color of dough which a child's grimy fingers have kneaded, an unhealthly hue that was repeated in his expressionless countenance.

He nodded, this Third Man, but made no other acknowledgment of what had been said to him.

"In the oil fields," Owl-Eyes began again, "it is as yet quiet. But Carlit has made plans for them."

"There they have not been easy to fool," Black Band took up the gambit just passed to him. "There are too few unreasoning laborers, too many skilled and intelligent workers, for the American agitators or our own emissaries to stir them up. In Texas, in California, I have started infiltrating my Green Shirts among them, have been establishing caches of rifles and machine-guns. They are yet too few, but in a month…."

"*A month!*" The Third Man's tones were soft and without inflection. "That is not soon enough by thirty days." They came from a wee rose-bud mouth so small as to be almost infantile, and issuing out of that tremendous bulk there was something—dreadful—about them.

"You two, Carlit, Horon, are too slow, entirely too slow, in your preparations. That is why I was sent here, that is why I hastened to this place as soon as I landed.

"We have drained ourselves dry, have poured gold into our sea fleets and our fleets of the air; into shells, and munitions, and gas. Today we are ready to strike, and you, you who for two years have had time to enfeeble this land, to stir up class against class, brother against brother, to prepare for our onslaught so that when we do strike there shall be no doubt of our quick and complete victory—you prate to me of months.

"Months!"

"Those oil fields must be aflame three days from now. The

railroads must be wrecked, the mines destroyed. Three days from now your Green Shirts must be on the move, for three days from now our airplane carriers will be within two hours' flight of the Eastern Seaboard, those of our allies as near the Western, and our leader will give the signal for hostilities to begin."

"But that is impossible," Owl-Eyes, Horon, jerked out. "We cannot be ready."

"The last contingents of Green Shirts are not sufficiently trained," Carlit groaned. "You have seen those I myself have drilled...."

"I have seen them," the Third Man responded, in that soft, terrible voice of his. "They are better trained than our soldiers. You will send them at once to that Texas of which you speak. You will give orders at once for the Green Shirts in the other centers across the continent of which you have told me to be on the move to their posts. You will have your transportation units begin at once the distribution of the munitions from your caches, like this one outside."

"At once...."

"And you will inforn everyone that the signal for them to go into action will be the appearance over them of the black-winged planes of our land. Three days from now America must be in flames."

"But," Carlit gasped, "our communications system has not yet been perfected. Once our forces begin moving, there will be no way to recall them. If the Leader should change his mind, should decide to delay...."

THE THIRD Man shot one grim look at Carlit, silencing the protest. Then he spoke slowly.

"The Leader cannot change his mind. He dares not delay. The women of our land are awake at last, the mothers.

"They point to their starving babies, their famished children and cry out against the Leader. 'We cannot feed them with gunpowder,' they cry. 'We cannot clothe them with the gray steel of your battleships. The coal they need to warm them is in the bunkers of your fleets, you grease the motors of your airships with the butter for the lack of which they die. We want no World-Empire, no conquests. We want milk for our babies. We want bread for them. We shall have them, if to gain them we must rend you limb from limb.'

"Their ultimatum lies on the Leader's desk. A week from now the mothers will be on the march, mothers enraged and battling for their children."

"A week!"

"Do you think any army in the world can stop a host of maddened mothers? Do you think anything can stop them if the Leader cannot say to them, a week from now; 'Here. Here are the wheat fields of America, the riches of the New World for your babies, and for their babies. You have starved that never again shall our people starve.'"

The others stared, silent.

"No? I thought not. Give the signal! You there at the wireless! Send the signal out!"

The pasty-faced man turned his head and looked questioningly at Carlit. Owl-Eyes nodded. The radio man's finger touched a switch and vacuum bulbs glowed into sudden light on the table. The finger moved again, reaching for the telegraph key that would send out a signal for America's destruction, a signal that could not be recalled....

The radio man slithered down in his chair, thudded from it to the floor. A fine, pungent mist followed him down, a mist that had jetted in that final instant across the room.

"Hold it!" husked from the partition door, flung open now. "Just as you are. Move a muscle and I let you have it!"

The shadow that had prowled the lean-to roof was poised, black, ominous, in the doorway. The blackness was that of an ebon-hued cloak enveloping a tensely vibrant form. A black felt hat was pulled low over a countenance faceless because it was completely hidden behind a stygian mask through which only eye-glint showed. One black-gloved hand was visible, menacing Carlit and Horon and the Third Man with the curiously thick-barrelled pistol from which the spray had jetted that had paralysed the radio operator.

The fingers that grasped the butt of that odd weapon were black. That which was curled about the pistols trigger was red, the red of spurting, arterial blood!

"Red Finger!" the Third Man gasped, staggering back a pace as if stunned by the sight of that scarlet digit, then freezing at a menacing dart of the thick-mouthed gun. "Red Finger!"

"Red Finger it is," the shadow's ghastly voice agreed. "The one man in America your schemers could not fool. Red Finger, here to greet the new ambassador from...."

"The second reason for my being sent here," the Third Man

interrupted. "The Leader has empowered me to offer the headship of his American Secret Service when we shall have conquered the United States, at a million dollars a year."

A short mocking laugh came from beneath the black mask.

Mask, robe, that scarlet trigger finger, were the badge of America's greatest counter-spy. Known only as Red Finger, he was execrated in half the chancelleries of the world. It might have been the blood of his country's enemies with which was dyed the digit that gave him his name, so many of them had died because of him.

"Your leader will never conquer the United...."

A noose, flicking out of the darkness behind him, closed on Red Finger's throat and choked the sentence off. Another went lower, pinioning his arms, in the same brief instant a hand, darting past his elbow, slashed his gas gun from his hand. He was caught at last! Red Finger was fairly caught at last!

THE THIRD MAN laughed, his great belly shaking jelly-like. "The one American we did not fool," he spluttered. "The great Red Finger."

The other two moved forward.

The counter-spy made no attempt at a fruitless struggle. He stood erect, seeming somehow supremely unconquered though the tight lariat cut into his arms, though he must be half-strangled by the noose on his throat.

"It was too easy," the Third Man chuckled. "When I stepped back at your so melodramatic entrance I stepped into the invisible beam of a photo-ray apparatus that alarmed the watchers at the door below. You did not think we conferred here blissfully without protection of any sort, did you?"

"No," Red Finger managed to push through his clamped larynx. "No."

There was no longer any humor in the Third Man's high voice, none in his face. "And so the career of Red Finger is over. My mission is indeed a success."

"Shall I let him have it now, Your Excellency?" The gruff question came from behind Red Finger. "I have a knife. I can slit him here, under the left shoulder, and he won't bleed at all."

The Third Man's wee mouth twitched. "No," he said softly. "Not just yet. First he shall watch us send the signal that means his country's end. Carlit. You can manipulate that wireless, can you not?"

"Yes, your Excellency," Black Band responded.

"Then go ahead."

Black Band turned, thumped stiff-legged toward the instrument....

"Wait!" Red Finger snapped. "Don't touch that key if you do not wish to die!"

Lashed and helpless as he was, something in the way he said that carried utter conviction. Momentarily at least. Carlit hesitated, half-turned....

The Third Man peered at the counterspy intently.

"I've got one of your Mills bombs in my other hand," Red Finger continued, "under this cloak. The pin is out and the lever is held down only by my thumb. If you move another inch I'll let go—and the explosion will set off all the bales of them on this floor."

"You lie," Carlit growled.

"Move and see.... You in back of me, I feel your knife against my back. Sink it, if you dare. A dead thumb will not hold the grenade lever down."

What little color there had been was drained from Owl Eyes' face. "You will be the first to die. There are thousands of bombs out there, they'll go off...."

"None of us will have to be buried," Red Finger agreed. "But that signal of yours will not be sent.

"No." His faceless head moved to the Third Man. "I did not imagine that your conference was unguarded. It was too easy for me to approach and eavesdrop on it, so I took my precautions. The game's up, Your Excellency, and you know it."

The Third Man blinked.

"What is it you wish me to do?"

Red Finger spoke briskly.

"You have a choice. Order your man Carlit to send a message I shall dictate, give me your parole of honor that Carlit and Horon will go back across the sea on the first available steamer, and remain there, and I will permit you to go to Washington and take up your duties as ambassador. Refuse, and I lift my thumb from the lever."

The fat-thickened lids slitted, so that the tiny eyes beneath them almost vanished. There was a moment of brittle silence, while the fate of two nations hung in the balance of one man's decision. Then:

"What is the message you wish sent?" the Third Man sighed. "It will be sent exactly as you wish." There was something magnificent in the way he accepted defeat.

Red Finger shrugged. "I shall be sure of that. I can read the code—in any language. Ready Mr. Carlit?"

Black Band nodded, his face purple with a rage that did not permit speech, his hand on the instrument's key.

"Here is the message. 'To all Green Shirt units wherever located. Our plans have been countermanded by the Leader.'" The whistling signal was clearly audible from the ear-phones that had been jerked from the operator's head as he fell. "'All previous orders are cancelled. Destroy all munitions caches. Destroy all weapons in your possession. Disband all units. By authority of the Leader's personal ambassador.'"

It was finished. The Third Man spread his gross arms wide, in a gesture almost pathetic. "What now, Red Finger?"

"Now," the shadow answered, "you will order these ropes removed from me and we shall go down, single file, out of this place, Horon carrying the radio man. Then I shall bid you good-bye."

The Third Man nodded slowly, gestured to Carlo and Horon, and led the way from the room.

Five figures slithered out of a riverfront alley's mouth, paused in the center of the wide cobbled street that was now deserted, though in a few hours it would resound with the roar of traffic.

"Where's Red Finger?" Horon inquired. "Where's...." His voice was drowned by a thunderous explosion, by a red flame spurting high into the heavens....

181

"I don't know where Red Finger went," the Third Man husked, "but there went the end of a dream of empire."

A WEEK after the events related herewith, Ford Duane stood in the door-way of his second-hand bookshop on Fourth Avenue. It was a glorious morning and even in that dusty thoroughfare the sun was a white glory.

Duane held a newspaper in his hands.

The headlines across its outspread page read; *Coal Mine Agreement Signed, Longshoremen Vote No Strike. President's Fireside Chat Hails Dawn of New Era of Industrial Good Will.*

Down near the middle of the sheet, just below the fold, a much smaller headline announced that a certain incoming ambassador to Washington, having presented his credentials, in a special interview had predicted a lessening of war tension.

And at the bottom of the page, a brief cabled dispatch from that envoy's country described the "return from maneuvers" of the dictator's armed aerial forces and the dispersal of their pilots and observers to civilian life....

A brief smile flicked across the gaunt bookseller's weary face and faded. He turned, and moved slowly to his desk.

A gray silk scarf was arranged in a swirl beneath the gooseneck lamp. On the scarf there rested a corrugated metal ball the size of a coconut, a tiny lever wired down to its surface.

THE SPY WHO SOLD DEATH

E VEN THE brilliance of the morning sun and the crisp,
tangy morning breeze, could not make the bookstall-lined
Fourth Avenue block other than a sluggish back-eddy of the
city's flood. Gray men dwelt sleepily here among their gray
books; men and books equally withdrawn from life. Elsewhere,
the eager day was beginning for thousands of school children,
stenographers and clerks, laborers and brokers, shopkeepers and
mechanics. Here the night's sleep yawned only into a waking
drowse, a desultory dealing in tattered volumes, a browsing
among out-dated magazines.

Elsewhere, life was vibrant, earnest; here it was a quiet flow of
featureless days. The booksellers of Fourth Avenue want only to
be left alone by a troubled world less real to them than printed
words on yellow, crumbling leaves. These Keepers of the Port of
Missing Books were, for the most part, gray old men.

Ford Duane, tall and gaunt, stooped under the weight of a
lassitude dreary as his dog-eared stock-in-trade, was not old,
but he was gray and droop-lidded and musty as the rest. He
lounged in the doorway of his store, his shabby alpaca smock
hanging loose from his lank frame, and to the chance observer
he seemed affected by a vast disinterest in anything save the
flicker of shadows on the sidewalk at his feet.

It would have taken a close observer, indeed, to have noted

that beneath their veiling curtains his gray eyes were sharply keen, that they flicked to every passer-by with a swift, almost terror-inspired sizing up.

It was impossible to see that within his enveloping smock muscles were coiled like steel springs, ready for any call, and that in its pocket was an unobtrusive weapon on whose instant availability Duane's very life might depend.

His life and, perhaps, far more than his life. Ford Duane was far other than he seemed. The quiet that lay about him was the brooding quiet of perpetual peril, that with which he dwelt was the eternal threat of death.

BEYOND THIS quiet street, beyond the hurly-burly of the awakening city, beyond the billowing ocean at the confluence of whose trackless highways it stands, the peoples of two Continents are arming and armed and trembling on the brink of war. Incident after incident, challenge after challenge occur, strife seems at last inevitable, yet at the final moment, at many final moments, it is averted. Strange that no one of these hot sparks sets the tinderbox of the Old World aflame? Yes, strange indeed, unless one comprehends that the balance of power and strength is equal balanced to a hairsbreadth, that there can be no hope of victory for either side, unless....

Unless the Giant of the West can somehow be induced to place its weight in one or the other scale. Unless unwilling America can, somehow, be drawn into the conflict.

To this end, an unseen army wages an invisible, continuous war between these far-flung coasts of ours, a war one against the other but both against our integrity, our reluctance to be embroiled in a strife that concerns us not. *Against* this end, a small but gallant company wages a secret defence. Unknown, unhonored, unacknowledged, devoted men toil to prevent the holocaust and disaster those other secret ones would bring upon us.

Of this invisible company Ford Duane was one.

Perhaps he was thinking of this. Perhaps he was recalling that in a dozen chancelleries there was a price posted on his head. Perhaps he was thinking only that it had been a month or more since a summons had come to him to prepare for special action against his country's secret enemies.

A SMALL boy went whistling along the sidewalk. A spate of traffic, released by the signal light's flick from red to green, surged between the curbs. A postman, blue-gray shoulder tugged down by his laden bag, trudged slowly toward Duane.

The postman turned in between the trestled boxes wherein were displayed *Bargains in Books* and nodded a good morning to the youth. He delved into his bag, handed Ford Duane a small package and retreated.

Duane turned the paper-wrapped bundle in his long, tapering fingers till the address was uppermost. Printed in a childish, unformed hand the return card told a message which only he knew—

From
Patricia Ann Thomas
Pattison
Austin Co., Texas

A muscle twitched at the corner of Duane's sharp jaw. There was no other sign that what he read had any meaning. But the initials, *P-A-T,* of the putative sender; the initials, *P-A-T,* repeated in her address, told him that there was a message contained in the package—perchance the very summons for which he had been waiting.

He tore the paper from it, there in full view of any who might be watching. He held up, plain in the sunlight, a belt woven from white beads, utterly without design.

Duane examined the belt in the sunlight, tried it about his waist. It was much too big. He pretended to laugh, turned and went into the gloomy interior of his shop. He went straight back between the high, dark bookstacks to a curtained opening in a partition at the rear, hooked the curtain back as he went through so that anyone who might happen to come in could see the unpainted wooden table within and the rumpled cot that marked the space as his living quarters. He tossed the belt on the table, carelessly, and it seemed only by accident that it fell flat. It was shadowy here and so only natural that he should turn on a two-socketed reading-lamp standing on the table. He did it quietly.

He threw himself on the cot, picked up a book that lay face down on it. He appeared to be reading the book but his look slid over its top and to the seemingly unregarded belt.

In the light from the lamp some of the beads glowed with a violet radiance of their own. Those which were thus fluorescent made an unsymmetrical pattern, thus:

The dots and dashes were in the Morse code, and Duane read them as fluently as though they were in the common alphabet. He read; "Foreign agent Room 3 Winston Hotel Determine identity T."

He reached out and twitched the strap from the table-top. A thread broke and the whole thing unravelled, the beads spilling to the floor. Duane heaved from his couch, looked ruefully down at the mess he had made, scratching his head.

A quarter hour later he was out on the sidewalk in front of his shop, was speaking to Otto Rumpf, the bearded, skull-capped owner of the bookstore next to him on the left. "I'm feeling rotten today," he said. "If you'll watch my place for me I'll go in back and lie down."

The man peered at him with bleared eyes magnified by thick lenses. "Ja," he growled. "Your lips are cracked und dere iss no color in your face. Go und rest. I vill tage care uff your shtore like mein own."

Duane returned to the small room in the rear and lay down again, pulling the blankets up over his shoulders and his head. The long form tossed for a while and then was still.

Ford Duane crawled out from behind the cot, glanced backward to it. The lumped sheets under the blanket looked very realistic. No one glancing through the half-curtained opening would have any reason to doubt that he still lay there. He

crawled to a side wall that could not be seen from outside and lifted to his feet. A touch of his finger on an excrescence in the plaster—and a panel slid noiselessly open to reveal a recessed niche. Duane went into the niche and the panel closed silently behind him.

THE WINSTON HOTEL'S cheap facade leared at the crowded Bowery block, each shuttered window a separate, significant wink. A creaking sign over the shabby entrance said: *Transients. Rooms $1.50.*

There were no questions asked of the 'transients' who patronized the Winston. They paid their buck and a half at the desk, strictly in advance, took their keys and climbed uncarpeted stairs to rooms indicated by the numbered tags. If they chose to have slinking, furtive visitors of either sex no one cared. If they didn't pay another buck and a half before nine in the morning they were requested to leave, none too politely. If they did pay, they were permitted to remain.

Stores on the ground floor left space only for the narrow lobby and the stairs, so Room 3 was one flight up level with the "El" station platform. Its shutters were tightly closed and the black shades drawn down, so that there was scarcely any light in it—and its three occupants were vague, shadowy figures.

Two of these figures, short, possessed of a curious litheness, were standing. The third was in a chair, bold upright with a strange rigidity, and his outlines showed him to be far bulkier than the others. The muffled sound he made was distinctly that of a throat trying to force words past a gag.

"Our friend seems to be not quite comfortable," one of the standing men said. "Perhaps you have bound him too tightly, Kusai, and the cords cut into his flesh." The words were precisely enunciated—too precisely to be pronounced by one to whom English was a native tongue—and an odd sibilance ran through them.

"He will not be troubled by it long," the one addressed as Kusai replied. "We will release him in just a minute." They were speaking to one another, these two, but each remark they made was patently a cruel taunt intended for their helpless prisoner. "Yet, he will remain here much longer than he expected."

"Yes. His precautions to hide himself will unfortunately be in vain. He will be found here by the police."

"But he will not know it, Hoan." Kusai's laugh was an inhalation of breath between tight lips. He turned to a scarred dresser against the wall, pulled one of the topped drawers completely out. There were papers in the hand he reached into the space from which the drawer had come, and there were none when it came out. "Do you think the police will surely find the documents where *apparently* he concealed them?" he asked as he replaced the drawer.

"Let it remain a little open, the papers preventing its shutting." Hoan was placing some objects on the rumpled bed—a tiny vial, a hypodermic syringe. "Are you certain that you have placed everything there?"

"Yes. His commission as agent of the *Ogpu*, genuine. A letter in Russian, forged, directing him to destroy the New York Subway. Giving the details, even to the time, of what we intend. Making certain that his nation will be blamed for the catastrophe."

"Very good. These cigarettes, with the damning circulars within their tubes, printed on rice paper, and calling upon the slaves of the Subway barons to rise, we shall place in his pocket, one broken so that its contents will be noted."

Again that hissing laugh from Kusai. He came back to the bound man and there was now a wadded rag in his hand, a rag from which came a queerly pungent odor. "You will feel no pain, my friend," he whispered, "and in a little while you will feel nothing at all." He placed the wad gently, almost tenderly, over the dimly seen nose and mouth.

The great body in the chair quivered. Biceps swelled against the tight cords, but they did not give. The chair creaked, but did not break. Hoan sighed. The big man slumped and was very still.

"In truth," Kusai remarked, "his name should be inscribed on the Tablet of the Honored Dead. Living, he was the Empire's enemy; dead, he will be its friend. But thanks to this invention of our honorable chemists he will not be gathered to his ancestors for another hour."

"Enough," the other snapped. "We have work to do. Unbind him."

It was done, deftly and swiftly. The two small men took a last look about the room, moved to the window.

Kusai lifted the shade, slowly, careful to make no sound. White light dotted the shutter beyond the open sash, probed through its chinks. Hoan felt of his pocket and a sly smile crossed his hairless, saffron countenance as a brass tag clinked against a key. Outside, there was the roar of a train coming into the station, the rattle of opening gates. The two killers waited.

Gates slammed and starting bells tinkled. Hoan touched Kusai's elbow, and the Oriental moved the shutter outward. The train was pounding into renewed motion. The upper half of a store sign jutted up across the cornice outside the window, so that Hoan could not be observed from below as he climbed out. The "El" platform's railing was only two feet from the sign, and the departing train had emptied it. Hoan leaped the space, was over the railing in a twinkling, was signaling to Kusai that the way was clear.

The latter went out on the cornice and squirmed around the shutter edge. It closed and the room was shadowed once more. Shadowed and very silent, for the space of thirty heart-beats. Then there was sound again in it, the scrape of metal against metal from the door, the click of a lock. The door slid open and a new form slipped in through the slitted aperture.

THIS MAN was tall, gaunt, slightly stooped. He wore a black hat whose wide brim turned down to conceal his face. He glanced swiftly around the room, seemed startled at sight of the inert body in the chair, crossed to it. Long, tapering fingers propped the chin of the moribund man, turning his face up to view. The intruder whirled, took in all of the room in a single darting glance, noted the jutting bureau drawer. He was at it, pulling it out, and fishing out the papers Kusai had placed there with a clumsy imitation of concealment.

Breath hissed between his teeth and the man was at the window, back to it, reading that damning letter. There was abruptly on the page a blaze of white light let in by the opening shutter. A saffron arm, muscular, steel-strong, whipped about the lean man's neck, and the shutter slammed closed again as Kusai leaped in to make his garroting hold good.

A storm of combat broke loose in that dim room, a savage battle the more weird because of the silence in which it was fought. There was no sound except the muted gasp of choked breath, the pad of rubber-soled feet on the carpeted floor.

Kusai's hold did not slip, but the lank man's elbow was driven back into the Oriental's belly so that the Mongol could not gain the leverage necessary to entirely cut off his antagonist's breath. The latter managed to half-twist and bring the pressure of that hold against the side of his neck instead of the larynx. His free hand dived into a pocket, flashed out with a strangely thick-barreled, flare-muzzled pistol.

The queer gun reached up to his shoulder, sprayed a fine mist over it. Kusai's grip relaxed, and suddenly he was a lax, inanimate bundle on the floor. The tall man loosed another burst of spray at him, pocketed the odd weapon, dropped to his side. The long fingers made a rapid search of the fallen Mongol's pockets, came out empty. It bothered him a bit.

"No evidence of who and what he is," the man muttered. "If they find him here, he will be imprisoned as a sneak thief. He will not come to in time to warn his comrades."

He stood up, glanced hurriedly at the letter again. A gray horror filled his face at what he read. He darted out of the room and locked it once more with the skeleton key that had afforded him entrance.

A SQUAT, saffron-complexioned man paced the platform of the Bowling Green station of the New York Subway. He was inconspicuous in a navy blue Homburg and an oxford-gray Chesterfield topcoat that might have been tailored on Fifth Avenue. He carried a small black bag, like a physician's, and he seemed to have an appointment with someone here, so frequently did he glance at his wrist watch.

With each stride up the platform he came nearer its downtown end, where the tracks curved into a tunnel whose roof was already rounding for the long passage under the East River. The rails pitched steeply downward for the curve was very deep.

Hoan reached the very end of the station just at the moment of ten. He slipped a key out of his pocket and dropped it there. The key's tag was stamped: *Winston Hotel, Room 3*. The Oriental glanced around, saw no sign of being watched, hopped down a set of four iron steps to the roadbed and was running at once down that steep incline into the depths of the river tube.

Ten is the time of change-over from the morning rush-hour schedule to the more leisurely time-table of the middle of the day. There would be only one train through the tube for thirteen minutes, and thirteen minutes was ample for what he had to accomplish.

The white tile of the station environs gave place to drab, whitewashed walls. The passage narrowed to a single-tracked tube. Hoan ignored the red and green signal bull's-eyes but he counted very carefully the spaced blue lights that mark off distances in the Subway. He knew exactly his objective, the point where the shoreline ends and there is over the tunnel only a hundred yards of silt and the—*river.*

Here it was, a niche in the side-wall making a place of refuge for a trackwalker trapped between trains. Hoan knelt in the recess, placed his bag on the ground, opened it very carefully. It was almost filled by an oblong steel box and within this there was enough of a certain explosive to smash the tube and let the river into the tunnel.

Hoan fished two coils of wire out of the bag, one end of each attached to opposite ends of the steel bomb. The free end of one he wrapped around the nearest rail, making sure that the contact was firm. From the lining of his coat, he drew a slender bamboo rod and fastened to its tip the free end of the second wire.

The rails were humming now, with the sound of an approaching train. Hoan shrank back into the recess, waiting for it to pass. When it had gone by he would reach out and touch the tip of the rod he held to the third rail.

The oncoming train sent its thunder before it. There would be nothing left of Hoan after the explosion. That was unavoidable. The whole carefully worked out scheme could not be left to the vagaries of any mechanism. Only the human hand was sure not to fail—only the hand of Hoan. Hoan had been very glad when that was decided. It was such an honor as few men merit, this opportunity to die in the service of the Emperor.

Kusai had been jealous. A banal role had been assigned to him, to remain behind to make certain that nothing interfered with the plant that would place blame for the disaster on the representative of the Ogpu.

This last moment of waiting was hard to bear, however, with sound deafening Hoan, with gale of that rushing train a tornado screaming across his niche. Moment? It was eternal. Something must have happened to the train. Hoan dared to peer out past the corner of the recess.

It was a juggernaut, red-eyed and green-eyed, roaring down upon him. A juggernaut he would destroy, hurling a tidal wave of waters after its thunderbolt when it had passed. A black splotch blotted its front—a monstrous black form on the little shelf projecting beyond the train's closed front door, a thing of black,

195

swirling draperies clinging to the little chains across the door with one black gloved hand, while another stretched out before it, clenching a queerly thick-barreled, flaring-muzzled pistol!

Hoan saw this great black man-bat in a flash, saw that the finger curled on the trigger of that weird gun was not black but scarlet. His own hand darted under his lapel, snapped out with a gun, and he was firing at the grotesque Thing.

The crack of Hoan's gun was lost in the thunder but he saw the black draperies jump to the bullet. Once more! Fine spray spat at him from Red Finger's weapon, spat into his brain. He went down, down into oblivion, but just as darkness claimed him he saw that black bat swoop from the front of the train—

"It didn't work, Hoan," a voice came from the grotesque shape. "There will be no torrent of indignation sweeping this land against the nation upon whom you planned to foist the blame for the outrage you schemed, sweeping it into war allied with your Empire and making certain the defeat of your Empire's enemy."

"Kill me, Red Finger," Hoan begged.

"No, Hoan. I shall not kill you. I shall let you go, and the secret of what you tried to do shall remain with me."

The Oriental rose to his feet. He turned and went totteringly off up the long slope of the Subway's tunnel. He went to death, despite the forebearance of him who had defeated him. To death by the sword of a samurai, inserted into the bowels in accordance with the proper ritual, in accordance with the immemorial rites of the hari-kari.

DUSK WAS creeping into Fourth Avenue when Ford Duane

came sleepily to the door of his shop. Weariness lined his face, but under his drooped eyelids there was a glint of content.

Otto Rumpf peered near-sightedly at him. "Ach," he quavered. "You look better."

"Yes," Ford Duane sighed. "I enjoyed my sleep. It was very restful. For sometime I should feel—at peace."

RED FINGER'S
MURDER MESSENGER

THE SHADOWS of a late spring dusk crept almost stealthily into that block of secondhand bookstores on New York's Fourth Avenue that is known as the Port of Ancient Books. From afar there came into its drowsy quiet a growling rumble compounded of the roar of traffic, the chatter of the mighty millions—all the tumult of the teeming city. Here, sound was limited to the soft slither of a rag lovingly dusting some rare volume, the rustle of sere pages under the hand of some browser at the sidewalk boxes trestled in front of the grimed windows of the shops, the scrape of feet as a shabbily dressed man shambled slowly down the sidewalk.

Ford Duane leaned against the doorpost of his store, that was different from the others in the block only because his name was lettered in scabrous gilt across its cornice. The drab alpaca smock, hanging loosely from his shoulders, cloaked a tall, loose-jointed figure. There seemed only lassitude in his gaunt, hollow-checked countenance, a vast disinterest in life.

Beneath Duane's drooped lids, his eyes watched with a fierce intentness the man who slowly approached. Every muscle in that apparently relaxed frame of Duane's was now gathered for instant action. So might a moving tiger have tautened with the drift of a shadow through the sunlit jungle—a shadow that might be merely a cloud drifting across the sky... or death crouching to leap upon him.

For to Ford Duane, buyer and seller of discarded tomes, human flotsam in this back eddy of life's stream, death, and worse than death, was a constant threat, eternal vigilance the price of safety.

The man whom Duane watched now shambled closer, peering at the shops as if he were searching for some particular establishment. His slow gait, and the stoop of his shoulders, did not come from age—for his face, faintly stubbled though it were, was that of one not far in his thirties. The horn-rimmed glasses, whose lenses were so thick they hid his eyes, the long hair fringing his ears, disorderly appearance of his worn clothing, stamped him as one of those accustomed to lurk in this abode of yellowed literature—a scholar to whom the search of knowledge is the only reality of life.

He came abreast of Duane's shop, turned and walked toward the tall bibliophile. Duane lifted away from the doorpost. "How do you do?" he said, before his visitor came too close.

The fellow paused. "You are Mr. Duane?" he asked, accents slurred and hesitant, "the bookseller?"

"Yes. At least, I am the Duane who keeps books and hopes that some one will buy them, occasionally. You are looking for me?"

"Yes," the other breathed. "I was told that if I want a book that is hard to find, you are the best man to come to."

"And you are looking for such a book now?" Duane prompted.

Stub-fingered hands fumbled at a pile of tattered magazines

in the box beside the student as the man gave its name, *"Pantagruel at Toulouse.* P. Atkins Townsend was the publisher, but he's no longer in business and the book is out of print."

Duane's expression did not change, but the pulse throbbed in his wrist. There was no such book, nor had there ever been such a publisher. In the title of that book and the name of the publisher, there was concealed a signal for Duane. Their initial letters were the same—P. A. T. In many forms, that signal had previously come to him. They were the credentials of messengers from the invisible head of the phantom organization to which Duane belonged. Each time messages, thus heralded, had come, it had meant that for a little while Ford Duane would be absent from Fourth Avenue. Later, after he had returned from his mission, some chancellery of Europe or Asia would cross off a name or two from a list of secret agents and some carefully worked out, secret political scheme would be marked, *Defeated!*

"Pantagruel at Toulouse?" the seeming shopkeeper repeated. "I may be able to get it. But I am not sure. Can you tell me more about it?" He was far other than he seemed, this lank, almost cadaverous individual.

Duane was a soldier in a war that knows no end—a mystery-cloaked, anonymous participant in the strife of spy and counter-spy, of saboteur and shadowy defender, that goes on eternally in a land that is at peace with all the world—and all the world *apparently* at peace with it.

"I am sure you have the book," said the stranger. "The person who sent me here told me he saw it on your shelves. Far to the rear, he said—he descried its location *perfectly.* If you will let me, I can show you exactly where it is."

"All right." If anything, Duane's face was blanker than before. He stepped aside, motioned the spectacled man past him. They went into dimness, moved between high stacks of books that exhaled the distinctive odor of yellowing paper, of moldering binder's cloth and worm-ridden leather, a musty smell like nothing else in the world.

"You have something to give me?" Ford Duane asked, low-toned.

"Yes," the man answered, and whipped around. "*This!*" Metal gleamed in the shadows—a knife flailing straight for the bookseller's heart!

IN FOURTH AVENUE the street lamps blinked on. The door of Ford Duane's Secondhand Bookstore opened, and closed again. A stooped man, wearing glasses with lenses so thick they hid his eyes, shambled past the box that held a stack of tattered magazines, and shuffled along the sidewalk toward the corner. He moved slowly, because he held an open book in his hands, seemingly reading it. In spite of his glasses, he was so nearsighted that he had to hold the book high—and it *concealed* his face.

The man's shabby clothing was too tight—as it should have been, not belonging to him. The frayed hem of his trousers exposed inches of untidy sock. He reached the corner, turned east. Then he slammed shut his book, and abruptly his long legs began to move rapidly. He reached Third Avenue and turned again, hurrying past the bedraggled shops and drab tenement

doorways of that thoroughfare. Halfway down the block, he ran up a broken-stepped stoop, shoved open a door scrawled over with the chalked obscenities of small boys and dived into a dark hallway which reeked with the stale smells of yesterday's corned beef and cabbage.

Another door creaked in the darkness. The man went down rickety wooden steps, across a debris-strewn cellar floor to a plank-walled cubicle that once had been a coal bin but now was a room which a hard-pressed janitor rented to a certain derelict for a dollar a week.

The rusted lock on the door of that cubicle was curiously intricate, yet it yielded at once to the man's key—then clicked shut behind him. In the tarry darkness, to which it admitted him, a bedstead creaked, and then there came a curious scraping of brick upon brick. After a minute, the sound was repeated… then absolute silence surged through that dark cellar chamber.

Now, the man had almost reached his goal….

The curtain in the wide aperture, cut through the partition at the rear of Ford Duane's Bookstore, was looped back. Anyone, looking in from the sidewalk, could see the wooden kitchen table, food-laden shelves, two-burner gas stove that revealed the space behind as Duane's living quarters—but not the whole space. They could not see the iron cot on which a prisoner now lay, bound to it by thin but exceedingly strong cords, his mouth gagged. They could not see this prisoner's eyes blink open and stare dazedly at the ceiling, as if his brain were still foggy. This prisoner was still unable to quite figure out why his knife had not gone home, in Duane's heart, why, suddenly, a fine mist had sprayed from out the very book stacks and somehow sending him down… down into oblivion.

The prisoner's head now jerked to a furtive slither. Against the rear wall—far enough to the other end of the room so that it could not be observed from out front—a black line abruptly marked the floor. It widened, as he caught sight of it, became a slit in the floor. Now the slit was a square hole out of which came a smell of damp, dank earth, as from a tunnel. Ford Duane's head came up out of the hole, his shoulders. This was his goal.

DUANE WAS up in the room. The panel had slid shut again, closing the hole out of which he had come. He seated himself in a chair and started stripping off the killer's suit he had been wearing.

"Come to?" Duane said, quite pleasantly. "You didn't get much of a dose—just enough to knock you out." Duane reached for his own clothing. "You gave yourself away by asking to be taken inside. All messages are delivered to me where everybody can see they're only books, or packages. I open them at once in full view, to demonstrate the innocence of their contents." He donned his smock, stood up to button it. "There isn't a foot of those shelves that isn't equipped with hidden nozzles that will spray forth a knockout gas of my own invention, if I shove my toe against the baseboard. You didn't have a chance of reaching me with your knife."

Duane crossed to his prisoner, stood above him, studying his face. With the glasses gone, it was no longer a scholar's countenance. It was beady-eyed, ratlike—showed only enough intelligence for murder.

"You didn't work out that scheme yourself," Duane went on. "Someone sent you to kill me. I'm going to find out who that someone is, and why. But first I shall close up shop. I can do that now because my neighbors, and any confederate of yours, who might have been watching from under cover, have seen you leave and so they won't wonder what has become of you. That's why I ran out there in your clothes."

The outside book-boxes he now took in, locking the store's front door. Duane padded back to the partition at the rear, unhooked the curtain and dropped it across the doorway. He moved to the cot, leaned over and unfastened the man's gag.

"Well," he said softly. "Who sent you?"

A stream of profanity spewed from the bound man's mouth.

Duane smiled without humor. He reached a long arm to the provision shelves on the wall, took down a bottle of clear liquid labeled, *Vinegar*. When he extracted its waxed cork, white fumes curled from its mouth.

The man on the cot was silent, his pupils dilating.

"I'm not particularly interested in getting revenge for the attempt on my life," Duane murmured. "But the way the attempt was made shows that some message to me has been intercepted. I want to know what that message was, and the people who sent you here can tell me. I intend to find out who they are, and what they are planning."

He tipped the bottle in his hand and let a drop of the liquid from it fall on the bedclothes, where his captive could see it. The wet place darkened, was black almost at once. And then there was no spot on the blanket at all… only a tiny, awesome hole.

"Nitric Acid," Duane explained. "Just think what it could do to—*your eyes!*" His free hand lashed forward, and his fingers, slim but exceedingly strong, were clamped on the killer's jaw, holding his head immobile. "Just think of the pain as it burns in. Just think of being blind, of being in the dark—always in the dark—till you die." The bottle hovered above the man's eyes. A glittering drop formed on its lip, quivering.

"I'll talk," the man shrieked. "Don't let it fall. For the love of God, don't let it fall. I'll talk!"

IN THE Eighties, between Broadway and Amsterdam, the old brownstone private houses have not yet been crowded out by towering elevator apartments. They have, for the most part, however, been turned into discreet lodgings—the comings and goings of whose tenants are never questioned as long as their rent is paid.

Lizzie O'Flaherty, the landlady of a certain one of these houses, considered herself singularly fortunate in having rented her whole parlor floor to two nice-looking foreigners who had paid a whole month's rental in advance. True, they seemed to have a lot of visitors, at all hours of the day and night, but there was never any noise from their quarters—so why should she bother her head about that?

Lizzie might have been interested, if she could have looked into the rear room of her parlor floor at about ten o'clock of the same night that Ford Duane had his unusual caller. But it would have been rather difficult, since the black blinds over its tall, deeply exnbrasured windows were drawn tightly down. The doors to the hall, and to the rest of the suite, were locked and double-locked.

The table in the center of the room was piled high with green, rectangular slips of paper. The papers, of a peculiar texture and peculiarly speckled with tiny, wriggly silk fibers, were bound into inch-thick bundles by wide paper bands. Each of these bands was imprinted with figures—*$500, $1,000.* There were a great many of them.

The chandelier in the high ceiling was none too bright. The walls were dark with the patina of age. The bulky furniture, the tall wooden wardrobe in the corner next to the windows, the wide sliding-doors in the wall opposite them, the carpeting on the floor, were battered and worn with the years. But that tremendous pile of money dominated the room so that all else in it seemed insignificant.

The two men, whom Lizzie O'Flaherty thought herself so fortunate to have as lodgers, now stood on either side of the table. One was taller than the other, and burly. His head was almost square in shape, his scalp was covered by short yellow hair upstanding and stiff as the bristles of a brush. His eyes were the exact blue shade of a bisque doll, but tiny evil lights glinted in them as though seized by intense inner excitement.

His companion was shorter, wiry, narrow, hawk-beaked countenance dark to swarthiness. His mouth was small and cruel, his hands corrugated by blue veins, their digits more like talons than fingers. One of these hands lay on the pile of bills.

"A half billion dollars, Maier," the little man said, slowly, gloatingly. "Not counterfeit, but printed on the government presses, from the government plates, on government paper, though never authorized by Congress." There was an elusive foreign intonation to his speech, each syllable clearly enunciated. "When our co-workers filter them, and all those others back in the warehouse, into circulation, what will happen to this nation that, despite its depression—despise the economic morass in which it struggles—still fatuously clings to its outworn democratic philosophy?"

A slow smile licked the blonde giant's thick lips. "Inflation," he answered, gutturally. "Prices of food, of the necessities of life, soaring beyond the reach of any but the most wealthy. The value of money falling—falling, like in my country it fell after the great war, till a handful of these will not to buy a postage stamp be enough. A half billion is not much against the wealth of America, friend Ciano, but, with all we also have in the warehouse, it will be enough to start disaster. That storm will roar on like the fires Vechkoff set two years ago in their forests of the north, till all over this proud land will be heard the cries of hungry children, moans of mothers, the trample and shouts of rioting mobs!"

"And then our forces shall spring into action, who have been gathered and trained for this purpose," Ciano took up the tale. "It has been so easy to fool these naive Americans, with sheets and hoods and secret passwords and shibboleth of patriotism— to swear them to unbreakable oaths of allegiance. Then our puppet will become—"

"Dictator of the United States," Maier broke in. "His name is already signed to the treaties that will extend to Washington the axis before which all Europe now quails in fear." He chuckled. "And so our great dream of a totalitarian state, embracing all the world, will come true. It has been easy to prepare the armed hosts who will bring this about. It will also be simple to get this money into the trade veins of an unsuspecting nation. Once out of our hands, whatever their Government attempts to quench the fire of inflation will be futile, for this is real money. Any doubt cast upon it will also cast doubt on all the other money of the land. But it was not easy to produce this half billion dollars and all the rest you have in the Balco warehouse. How was it accomplished, Ciano?"

The dark man's smile was almost lewd in its slow crawl across his face. "There are secrets of the East that we with white skins will never be permitted to know." He shrugged. "It was not hard to drug the sentries who guard the Bureau of Printing and Engraving in Washington, or to steal these plates—not with our system. It is too late for them to do anything about it. Too late, for, as you say, doubt cast on this money will cast doubt on all money—and thus the value of all America's currency will be destroyed."

"Too late," Maier licked his chops. "After midnight, when my men come for these bills, and those at the Balco warehouse, and scatter them all over the country, it will be too late to save Amer—"

"But it's not too late yet!" The sound of a shade ripping rasped across the hollow belly-voice that said this.

Maier and Ciano whirled to it, saw a black swirl come through the vertical slit in the blind and drop lightly to the floor.

"See how high you can reach, my friends," the voice said, and the apparition straightened, its black cloak swirling about it and making it shapeless.

It was faceless, too. Its broad-brimmed black hat shadowed

RED FINGER

only a gray, featureless mask, so that it seemed a sudden specter
of dread that jutted a curiously thick-barreled pistol at Ciano
and Maier. Stark rigid, their countenances quivering and yellow-
white as dough, they lifted trembling arms above their heads.
The hand that held that gun was black-gloved... except for the
finger curled on its trigger. *That* finger was scarlet as spurting
arterial blood.

Stark terror flared into Maier's eyes. "Red Finger!" spewed
from his colorless snout. "It's Red Finger!"

RED FINGER! That name is not known to the millions
who go about their business in America, peaceful and secure.
But to the man known as Red Finger, more than to any other,
they owe their peace and security. Among the gray, whispering
cohorts of the invisible army that eternally gnaws to undermine
American institutions, the name Red Finger is a name of fear.
Many of them have met and seen him in this fearful guise, but
few have lived to creep back to those who had dispatched them
on some evil mission against the United States!

"Red Finger," the grim voice repeated. "But why not give
me my real name? You know it, Anton Maier, do you not? You
sent an assassin to dispose of me not many hours ago. You really
thought that I could be knifed and left weltering in my own
blood."

"I thought..." the German fluttered, "I thought...."

"If you had thought, you wood not have revealed to me that
you know who I am." The masked man moved slowly toward
the trembling couple, a relentless, weird apparition in his swirl-

210

ing black robes, an avatar of gruesome doom. "For, because of your knowledge, you both must die."

Through the aperture out of which he had come now could be seen a pane of glass swinging from a cord taped to it and fastened to some hook in the outer wall. Red Finger had sliced it cleanly, without sound, from its sash. But there was no fire-escape ladder out there—only a sheer drop of twenty feet of brick wall to the backyard beneath. He must have climbed that twenty fet by clinging, flylike, to the bricks itself.

"You must die," Red Finger repeated, coming alongside the table, and to the right of it, "even before I…."

A hand darted past his right side, slashed his weapon from his grip. "It is you who must die," a peculiarly crisp voice said, "Mister Ford Duane." The squat, saffron-faced, slant-eyed individual who had slipped out of the wardrobe, as Red Finger had passed it—then come up noiselessly behind him—twisted his automatic muzzle into the counter-spy's spine. "No longer will you interfere with the destiny of the stronger races of mankind."

Maier's arms came down, and he shook with silent laughter. "Good work, Yamikoto," he chuckled. "You see, my dear Red Finger, we know your methods. We knew that you were spying upon our plans. So very openly we talked, that you would feel sure we did not suspect your presence. Your caution lulled, you have revealed yourself. But, all the time, little Yamikoto in the closet was concealed, awaiting you."

"In other words," Ciano put in. "We baited a trap for you and you walked into it quite blithely. Too bad. You were the only American we feared, and with you out of the way all the zest will be gone from our great adventure. Yet the destiny of the world demands your death. No man, however admirable he may be, can be permitted to break the triangle that henceforth will rule the earth's destiny—Europe, Asia, and America."

"You understand," Yamikoto put in, "why I regretfully must pull trigger? One minute you may say prayer and then…. What that?" he broke off to exclaim sharply. "What is that smell…."

He was answered by a sudden brilliant flare of flame from the piled bills—a burst of fire that leaped about Red Finger. Red Finger dropped instantly, and rolled under the table. His strange weapon went with him, snatched somehow from the floor as he rolled.

"Your man told me a little more than you expected him to," Red Finger shouted. "I came prepared. You forgot to watch my left hand, spraying a solution of phosphorus in benzine over the bills!"

There came a curious, plopping sound—a spray of white mist into the glaring light of the blaze. The mist enfolded Yamikota, and the Asiatic, bending over to get a shot under the shielding table, thudded down, senseless.

Maier and Ciano, beating at the flames, were frantically trying to stem the fire that was consuming a half billion dollars. They did not hear the double plops from beneath the table, did not see the mist spurt again and envelope them. They folded down to the floor… were very still.

Red Finger rolled out into the open, his black robes fluttering with yellow tongues of flame. He grabbed up Yamikoto's automatic. The thud, thud, thud of his three shots were drowned by the roaring voice of the fire. And then he was tearing the mask from his face, the burning cloak from his body. Now to notify the police of that money stored in the Balco warehouse. It would be found, all right!

IT WASN'T till after the chugging engines had put out the fire in Lizzie O'Flaherty's lodging house, and the three bodies were found in the back room of her parlor floor suite, that anyone thought to wonder at the tall, lank man who aroused the house before escape was cut off, and how he could possibly have seen the flames from the sidewalk whence he appeared to have come. But by that time he had vanished....

The Balco raid took place a half hour later. It was completely successful.

It was just about that time that Ford Duane pounded on the door of the store of his neighbor on Fourth Avenue. When old Naismith opened up for him, he saw that Duane's face and hands were badly burned.

"Phone for a doctor," Duane gasped, reeling against the jamb. "I was frying some potatoes on my stove and the oil caught and flared up all over me." Then he folded, sliding down along the jamb to lie inertly on Naismith's threshold.

"Tsk, tsk, tsk," old Naismith clucked, dragging Duane's unconscious body inside. "Beats all how this new generation can't stand a little pain. Why, I remember when I was on the farm, I near cut my arm off with an ax and walked a mile to the doctor for help. Here's this boy, with just a few burns, and couldn't get more'n a couple yards from his backroom to my door without passing out!"

He never suspected the truth!

RED FINGER AND
THE MURDER TRIO

VIVID-GREEN PAINT, a searchlight mounted in the center of its stream-curved top, glittering letters on its hood, marked the streaking roadster as a police car. It slewed around a corner into Fourth Avenue, its siren howling with a curious incongruity through the dim quiet of that grimy block which is known as the Port of Missing Books. The ominous sound wailed into the hush of Ford Duane's Secondhand Bookstore, and the thick, dark shadows between towering tiers of tattered tomes quivered with a tense apprehension of dread.

Duane—gaunt and cadaverously lank, and stooped under the weight of a lassitude dreary as his stock-in-trade—appeared utterly oblivious of the pulse-stirring sound. But the pencil in his long, slim fingers halted, abruptly, in its idle tracing of a rose on the dust-filmed blotter covering the desk in whose chair the bibliophile slouched. Beneath their covert of drooped lids his eyes slid to an apparently accidental aperture in the window display, that gave them a clear view of the sidewalk. And of anyone who might seek entrance to the store.

Eternal vigilance was the price Ford Duane paid for life itself! He was not, by far, the defeated dealer in discarded books that he seemed.

The green car's bonnet surged into range of his vision, skidding to a sudden halt. The siren-howl crescendoed to a banshee shriek—and cut off! In the shattering silence heavy heels thumped on the concrete outside, and Duane saw a hulking, barrel-chested police sergeant lurch across the sidewalk, coming directly toward his own door.

The pencil snapped, broken in two. The hand that had held it darted under the desktop, closed on a concealed rubber bulb that if pressed would spray the space in front of the desk with paralyzing mist.

The door slammed open, and the cop pounded in. He jerked around to Duane, thrust a blue-hued, rocky jaw at him. "Yuh Ford Duane?"

"Yes." No change in the shopkeeper's lined countenance, no tremor in his drawl, betrayed his taut alertness. "What is it?"

"Inspector Collins wants ter see yuh."

Lids still wearily half-closed, Duane checked the man's appearance; his chevrons, the material of his uniform, the thickness of his shoes' soles. "I don't understand," he murmured. Every detail was meticulously correct, but that proved nothing. If his disguise had been penetrated, his sanctuary unearthed; if this were a ruse to carry him off to some lair where his enemies could work their will with him; no minutest item would be permitted to imperil the scheme's success. "What would Inspector— er— Collins want to see me about?" In the secret Game Duane played, the opponents do not underrate one another.

"Mebbe about a skirt called Stone," the sergeant growled. "Know her?" He abruptly bellowed. "Rose Stone!"

Rose! For half the instant a lightning flash takes to dart between cloud and earth the bookman's poise was shattered.

215

His glance flicked to the drawing on the desk, flicked back to the policeman. A pulse throbbed in his temple.

"Rose Stone," he repeated, puzzledly. "The name seems familiar—but I can't place it."

"Can't place it, huh?" The officer's gross lips pulled away from his teeth in a snarl. "Mebbe yuh'll place it when.... Hell! My orders is to bring yuh in. Comin' peaceable or do I have ter take yuh?" His hand slid under his coat, reaching for his holstered gun.

Duane's fingers twitched on the bulb they held. Their slightest pressure would render the man blind and helpless—would give the bookseller time to reach the secret exit from the store and vanish. He could assume another personality and—

But he unfolded his lean length from the broken-back chair. "I don't suppose I have any choice. I'll lock up and go with you." He shrugged, shambled out with the blue-clad man who might be a police officer....

Or a messenger of doom.

The roadster leaped away from the curb, seethed through traffic halted by its blaring siren. Poignant speculation seethed through Ford Duane's brain as, seated beside the supposed sergeant, he hurtled toward the unknown.

What had the cop meant, flinging that name at him? Rose! The rules of the Game say that the players must remain unknown to one another, team mates as well as antagonists. But Nature scoffs at manmade rules, and men and women cannot forswear human emotion. A face that for months had not been long out of Duane's thoughts hovered before him. A sweet mouth, formed for kissing. Gray, brooding eyes. Tawny hair in which light glinted duskily. He knew her only as "Flower." Once she had sent him a russet rose as token that she was alive, and safe, when he had feared her otherwise. A *rose*....

Was Rose Stone, Flower? Had that name been notice to him that the girl was a captive, her release offered in exchange for his own voluntary surrender?

The green car surged through gathering dusk that was like the eternal twilight in which the Game is played, the secret war between spy and counterspy, between phantom soldiers of phantom armies who know no truce, no armistice. Night was at hand. It might be Ford Duane's last night. Of all the men and women who—unknown, unhonored, unacknowledged—fight for America, he was the ace. In half the chancelleries of Europe there was a price on his head, and there were many who needed no regard to whet their thirst for his death....

But it was not love of country that carried him now into what might be deadly peril. It was love of a woman.

Brakes squealed. The car rocked, its flight suddenly ended against a gray curb. An iron band tightened around Duane's forehead. This was no police station from which a canvas canopy jutted. He read the name on a bronze plaque alongside the doorway. "Dolly Madison Hotel." Queer! The Dolly Madison took only women as its guests....

"Come on," the policeman grunted, already out on the sidewalk. "Get going."

The quiet lobby was feminine as the inn's name, hushed and decorous as the lonely gentlewomen who occupied its chairs in a patient, spinster solitude. But the hatchet-faced woman behind the clerk's counter seemed pallid, distrait, as her gimlet eyes followed the two who went past her; and the elevator girl fumbled nervously at her lever. The lift doors grated open. Duane followed his guide down a silent, camphor-odored hallway. The cop knocked on a numbered door at its far end. A key rattled in its lock and it opened.

The musty room was filled with men, broad-shouldered, husky, some uniformed, others in cits. Velour drapes stirred, languidly, in a draft coming through the open window. There was a day-bed against one wall. A table at the room's center was cluttered with books, an ink-stand and pens, a sheet of paper that had been written on. But that which drew Duane's look was a chair set before the table. A thin blanket had been thrown over that chair, and its pale blue was shaped to the outlines of a form. Of a slender, human form, ghastly in its immobility.

"This is Duane, Inspector," the sergeant who had brought him here said. "I got him here quick's I could."

Inspector Collins was one of the men in civilian clothes. His eyes were gimlet-sharp under their beetling gray brows. "Duane," he growled. "Come here." He stepped to the chair that held a grisly burden, and his one gnarled hand closed on the edge of the blanket, where it folded limply over the gruesome suggestion of a head forever stilled. "Come here."

The other men moved apart, making a path for Duane. There was something feline in the way they watched him. They seemed ready to pounce, to claw. But the book dealer was scarcely aware of them. He knew only that a corpse was hidden under that incongrously cerulean pall, and that in another second he would see its face. His throat was dry, a dull hammer thumped his skull. But his expression showed only bewildered curiosity, a timid wonder at the grotesque proceeding.

He stood above the shrouded body. "Who is this?" Collins barked, and jerked the blanket away.

She was slender, utterly feminine, in the big chair. One slim hand was clutched to a shirtwaisted breast, as though to repress a twinge of pain. The other lay in her lap, ink-splotched, its dead fingers tight on a pen. Duane forced his eyes upward—to a small, pallid chin, to a face gleaming with death's waxen pallor—

To a face utterly unknown to him! Breath hissed sharply from between his teeth.

"No." His voice was tight, thin. A cloistered seller of old books would be expected to be appalled by the sudden sight of death. Of murder! A dribble of blood had dried on the woman's cheek, blood that had trickled from a tiny black hole beside her right eye. "No. I have never seen her before."

"Sure?" Collins demanded. "Are you sure?"

"Of course. Why should I lie?" Duane watched Collins cover the woman again with the pale blue, fuzzy shroud, "Why did you expect me to know her?"

"She was writing a letter to you when she was shot. There it is, on the table." The police inspector gestured. "She registered here a week ago, but she had nothing to do with anyone in the place, was out most of the time. We've teletyped an inquiry to her home town, but those hicks are slower than hell, and I was sure we could get something out of you."

Duane was looking at the letter. He knew better than to offer to touch it, but he could read it. With the first lines he was keenly alert again behind his expressionless mask.

There was the date, his name and address in a formal heading. And then:

"Dear Sir:
Would it be possible for you to secure a copy of 'Pantagruel at Toulouse?' P. Atkins Townsend was the publisher, but he is out of business and the book out of print."

(Pentagruel *at* *T*oulouse! There was no such book. *P. A*tkins *T*ownsend. There was no such publisher. But the curious correspondence of the initials of the two names was no coincidence. P-A-T! Those three letters were the sign-manual of the players of the Game. They were a signal to Duane that he was about to receive a message intended for no one but him. The message must be hidden in the letter itself. It had been intended to be mailed. Was it concealed in the wording? Or written between the lines, in invisible ink? Much depended on that. How much he could not know, but the writer had been murdered to silence her. He would never be permitted to take the letter away from her).

"Whether or not you can do this," it went on, "the following list of books, at the prices quoted from your catalogue," (He had issued no catalogue. A tiny muscle twitched in Duane's gaunt cheek.) "and send them express collect to the Memorial Library at Raneville, Orange County, New York. Please note the prices, as the Board will pay no more."

(The prices! Were they the key to the message? Had the woman, hard-pressed, been compelled to invent a code on the spur of the moment?)

Alexander the Great, Wheeler	2.09
Departmental Ditties, Kipling	1.07
Elmer Gantry, Lewis	1.11
England Speaks, Gibbs	1.14
European Journey, Gibbs	1.06
Froissart's Chronicles	1.26
Foam of South Seas, Middleton	1.28
Idylls of the King, Tennyson	1.27
If Winter Comes, Hutchinson	1.17
Kipling Pageant	2.10
New Poetry, Monroe	1.18
Noyes' Poems	1.22
Odet's Plays	1.12
On Heroes, Carlyle	1.03
Other People's Money, Brandeis	.21
Outline of History, Wells	3.25
Poe's Works, Complete	4.02
Red Rover, Cooper	1.15
Shelley's Poems	2.01
Stars Fell on Alabama, Carmer	2.19
Thaddeus of Warsaw, Porter	1.29
The Conquest of Space, Lasser	1.05
The Last Puritan, Santyana	2.04

"I enclose a check for...." And then there was an ink-splotch, dragging down off the paper's edge. The same splotch was on dead fingers under a pale blue pall....

The door opened to admit a pot-bellied, vandyked little man, carrying a small black satchel and puffing fussily. "Sorry I'm late," he gasped. "I was in the middle of a thoracicotomy when your 'phone reached the hospital. Beautiful operation. Beautiful." He set down the bag on the day bed, rubbed his pudgy hands.

"Pulled the guy through, eh, doc," Collins responded. "Here's one you won't pull through."

"No. Patient kicked off. Bum heart. But it was a beautiful operation. What have you got here?"

"Dame plugged in the head. We figure she was shot from across the court." Collins jerked a thumb through the window, to a white painted wall fifty feet away, in which there was another open window. "Check on the bullet angle first, will you, before we move her?"

"Sure." The medical examiner opened his bag, and gleaming instruments jingled. Collins dragged the blanket from the corpse.

"Pardon me," Duane ventured. "May I make a copy of this

order? I should hate to lose it. The Raneville Library is my best customer, and...."

"All right," the Inspector interrupted, testily; "And then you get out of here." His lips curled with faint distaste.

The physician moved toward the cadaver, a silver probe in his hand. Ford Duane became oblivious of the ghoulish proceedings behind him. He was copying the list of books. But he wasn't copying it in the alphabetical arrangement the slain woman had made. His list began thus:

Shelly's Poems	2.01
Poe's Works	4.02
On Heroes	1.03
....	

He had solved the puzzle! The prices were indeed the clue, the cents part of them. There were thirty titles and there were thirty amounts, from one to thirty. The alphabetical arrangement had been camouflage.

He wrote rapidly, finished his list:

... Idylls of the King	1.27
Foam of South Seas	1.28
Thaddeus of Warsaw	1.29
Years Between	.30

and rose to his feet. "I'll be going now, if you don't want me any more."

No one paid any attention to him. The telephone rang, and one of the men answered it. Duane reached the door....

"Hell!" the man at the 'phone exclaimed. "Inspector! Raneville says they ain't got no library. That guy said they was his best cus...."

Ford Duane went through the door, slammed it, whirled around. The key that had been on the inside of the keyhole stabbed into it from outside, clicked over. A heavy body pounded against the panel, and a muffled voice roared from within.

Duane darted down the corridor that was filled with the sound of savage battering against the door he had locked, savage sound pursuing him. They would batter down the door in moments. They would 'phone downstairs to hold him. He saw a red light over a transomless portal, jerked the blind door open, pulled it shut behind him. He was on a firescape platform from which iron stairs slanted down within a long vertical recess in the hotel. Far below there was an areaway....

The stooped man who slouched, seconds later, out of that alley was grimy-faced, collarless. A gray, tobacco-stained mustache stragglingly hid his mouth, his eyes were red-rimmed, bleary, his gray hair unkempt. He had a newspaper-wrapped bundle under his arm, hugged close to an ash-smeared shirt. If Ford Duane had decided to duck out of his store his personality would have been changed as soon as he had been free of it. The necessity for that change had now arisen, and, as always, he had been prepared for it. The sergeant of police who burst out of the Dolly Madison's entrance, gun in hand, did not give him a second glance.

As the seeming hobo slouched away, his mind was busy with the letter a woman had written with death hovering over her.

As he had rearranged them, the first letters of the book titles had read;

SPOTTED TAKE OVER WINSTON TWO FIFTY

She had been on a case, had realized that her antagonists had discovered her identity. They were closing in on her. She had, doubtless, seen the slayer watching her from across the court-yard, had known she would never leave the room alive. She had written the message with some desperate hope of its reaching him, had not dared to take the time to be more specific. But she had expected him to understand.

He was to take over the investigation. "Winston." Some place in New York. A garage? A theatre? No. It must be a hotel. The "two fifty" was a room number.

The police would be watching the bookshop on Fourth Avenue against his return. But Ford Duane had other lairs in the city. He visited them seldom, under the pressure only of dire necessity. But in each one there was concealed all the appurtenances of disguise; maps and directories of the city....

And certain curious weapons that were curiously effective. **THE DOLLY MADISON HOTEL,** prim, prudish, would have drawn its respectable skirts away from contamination by the Hotel Winston. The latter's sleazy façade leered at the crowded waterfront block, each separate, close-shaded window a significant wink. A creaking sign over the shabby entrance said: "Transient Rooms $1.50."

There were no questions asked of the transients who patronized the Winston. They paid their dollar and a half at the desk, in advance, took their keys and climbed creaking stairs to the rooms indicated by the numbered tags. If they chose to have slinking, furtive visitors that was their business, and no one's else.

The three men and the one woman in Room 250 would not have been there had it not been for this convenient lack of curiosity. There would have been, almost anywhere else, an inconvenient curiosity as to the gathering together of a Negro, a squat big cheek-boned yellow man, and a white couple.

"Ah tailed heh to heh hotel, Misto' Krasnitch," the colored man, simian-armed, gorilla-faced, was saying. "But ah couldn't get in 'cause it wuz de Dolly Madison an' dey don't have nothin' except women he'p dere. Ah done spotted heh room, dough."

"Only women! The Dolly Madison, eh." There was only the trace of a foreign intonation in Krasnitch's accents, but his swarthy countenance, his tight cap of wiry hair, stamped him as an alien. A cold, cruel light smouldered in his deep-set eyes. "Lola will have to get on the job then."

" 'Taint no need," the Negro grinned. "De job's done."

"What do you mean, Jones?"

"De Moorish Ahms is nex' doah. One uv ouah comrades is a pohteh deh. An' deh wuz an empty flat right crost de couht f'om heh room. She wuz writin' a lettah an' we got a good shot at heh." He chuckled. "She neveh knew whut hit heh."

"A letter!" Krasnitch jumped up. "You fool! Maybe it was her report. The police will find it...."

"Noah feah. I done read it wit' my spy glasses. It wuz about a lot of books...."

"If our august comlades will pardon me," the Mongolian put

in, "I will lemind them that the wise man, having su'mounted an obstacle, leaves it behind him!" His liquid tones were low, soft, but the others were instantly silent when he spoke, instantly attentive. His long fingernails tapped on the table with a snapping sound. "Let us finish with the business which ou' discovely that we we'e spied upon intellupted, and dispe'se. The flea escapes the dog's claws because he bites and leaps away."

"Heh, heh," Jones chuckled. "The flea jumps... that's good!"

"But fi'st," the Oriental continued, smoothly. "I must ask who this woman is. I have not met he' befo'."

"She's all right, Ho Chien. Marie Rachnikov feared she was watched and sent a representative. I have checked Lola Sarnoff's credentials."

"Ve'y well," The Mongol seemed satisfied. "Then we may plocede. As I unde'stand it, we are leady. You, Ivan Klasnitch, have reported that the Slavic wo'kers in the steel mills and mines ah plepa'ed."

"That's right. They'll quit work the minute they're told."

"And you, Mees Lola. You speak fo' the female opelatives in the facto'ies. They are leady fo' a gen'al strike?"

"They are ready." Her voice was throaty, deep chested. There was a drowsy volupuousness about her that was as seductive as the stretch of a tigress, and as infinitely dangerous.

"And you, Washington Jones?"

"Mah folkses is allus ready to go on strike. Dey'll do just whut ah tells them."

Ho Chien's fingernails rasped on wood, as though he clawed some helpless victim. "Good! America is at our me'cy, com'ades, as Flance was at Ge'many's mercy last June, when he' labole's folded thei' a'ms. Flance, despite her a'my, ent'enched in thei' implegnable fo'ts, capitulated to Ge'many then, and fo'ced England to remove the sanctions against Italy. She knew he'self helpless, for today the real a'mies are not the soldie's at the flont, but the insignificant, sco'ned common labole's in the lea'. Flance was lucky, fo' he' enemies wele not wise enough to move when the moment was lipe. My Empelo' is wiseh." He rose, half-turned to the door. "I go, comlades, to let him know what you have done. Within twenty-fou' hou's he stlikes."

"No!" Lola, too, was on her feet, lithely. A gun snouted magically from her little hand. "Nor in twenty-four years." Her weapon seemed to cover all three at once. "Hands up, all of you. Your game's up."

The conspirators' arms rose above their heads. "What's this?" Obun grunted. "What kind of game are you playing?"

"The same kind that you are, but I've won." Lola's left hand jerked toward the blinded window. "There's a dictograph out there that's recorded every word you've said. I let it down from the room above before I showed up here. And now I'm calling the Department of Justice office in the Custom House." She reached for the telephone on the table, her eyes unwavering on the three statuesque men she had captured. "They can get here in fifteen minutes, and...."

"Find you—," Ho Chien's arm swept down. A metallic flash streaked across the room. A knife quivered, point inches deep in Lola's gun hand. "But not us." The girl's weapon thumped to the floor. Krasnitch, Jones, leaped, had her pinned helpless between

228

them. Her sick eyes watched the blood well from around the knife-blade, but no sound came from her gray, tight lips.

"A silent woman is dangelous," Ho Chien murmured, imperturbably. A faint smile of triumph touched his bluish lips, vanished. "When I noticed that she spoke only when spoken to I slipped my knife into my sleeve, to be leady fo' what was su'e to come."

"Gawsh," Jones licked his lips. "What we gonna do now?"

Ho Chien shrugged. "You have killed one woman today, A'e you averse to killing anothe'?"

"But they'll heah me shoot. Dat ain't no...."

"The succulent bamboo shoot may be flied as well as loasted. That knife has not lost its keenness because it haf dlunk blood once."

"Ah gets yuh." White teeth gleamed in the black face, and black lids narrowed with sadistic anticipation. Jones' bananalike fingers closed on the knife-handle, jerked it out of the wound.

Krasnitch's hand on her mouth, stifled Lola's cry of agony. The Negro ran a loving thumb along a razor edge.

"Beneath the bleasts," Ho Chien lisped. "She will not bleed much, the'e, and we can lay he' in the bed, cove' he' up with the sheets. She will be thought to be sleeping."

The glittering knife lifted. Its thirsting point slit the tight-stretched silk of Lola's dress, pressed against white, quivering skin.

The window sash thumped up in its frame! A black swirl bellied the shade inward. There was a fifth figure in the room, a startling, ominous figure, cloaked in swirling black draperies that made it incredibly tall, incredibly ominous.

"Drop that knife," a sepulchral voice intoned. "Drop it!" The apparition was gray-masked, topped by a gray felt hat. It was a specter of sudden dread. A pistol with a curiously thick barrel jutted from a hand that was gloved in black, except for the one finger that curled about the strange weapon's trigger. That was scarlet, hideously scarlet as the finger of doom.

"*Led Finge*," Ho Chien exclaimed, his Oriental stolidity shattered. "*Led Finge*!"

"Red Finger is right," the intruder echoed. "Get your hands up, way up, all of you." The name the Mongol had uttered was one of terror in the subterranean world where the endless war is fought. Ace of counter-spies, the bravest of America's secret enemies trembled at the very thought of him. Many had died at his hands, many had limped home to tell of failure at the moment of success. But he wore no medals. He was on no Roll of Honor… and never would be.

Jones' knife clattered to the floor, and his face was a livid green as he lifted his arms. Krasnitch's shook above his head in panic-inspired ague. Ho Chien's clawed hands lifted, slowly.

"Got enough guts to search them, girlie?" Red Finger asked. "I don't want to get too near them."

"Yes," the girl breathed, forcing a smile. "Yes, Red Finger." She shuddered, like someone coming out of a nightmare, turned. Her hands were suddenly deft as they took a short-barreled automatic out of the Negro's shoulder-holster, a blue revolver from Krasnitch's pocket, and tossed them into a far corner. She crossed to Ho Chien. Reached under his jacket.

The yellow man ducked. His snake-like arms wound around the girl, lifted her. Her frail body covered his, was a shield against Red Finger's bullets.

"Stop that!" the counter-spy snapped. "Drop her."

"So solly," the Oriental lisped. "Not to oblige." He backed toward the door. "So solly acquaintance with so famous individual must be so sho't." Lola was rigid, strengthless, in his fierce grip.

Jones laughed, cackling. "Golly," he chattered. "He'm gettin' away."

"Shoot," the girl screamed. "Shoot! Never mind me."

The scarlet finger twitched, A spray jetted from Red Finger's gun, a spray of fine mist that reached across the room, that enveloped Ho Chien in a hazy cloud. The Oriental thumped down, atop his unwilling burden.

The scarlet finger twitched again—and again. Krasnitch, Jones, were flaccid, motionless hulks on the floor. The black-cloaked man hurled himself across the room, stooped and lifted the girl with effortless strength. His free hand darted inside his cloak, came out with a wet sponge. He slapped it on her nostrils.

A wig lay on the floor, alongside Ho Chien's sleeping form. The girl's hair was russet now, the yellow light glinting tawny in its lustrous tresses. Her arm crept up, crept around Red Finger's neck. Her lids trembled, opened on gray eyes that peered into the slits in Red Finger's gray mask through which keen blue eyes peered anxiously.

"Flower!" the suddenly quivering counter-spy husked. "How did you…?"

"I didn't know anyone else was working on this case. You know how Headquarters is sometimes. Check—and double-check. But they didn't need to—with you."

"Headquarters doesn't know I'm on it—" Red Finger was abruptly conscious of the soft, yieldingly warm body in his arms, of the heart thumping in his arms. He shoved up his mask. His lips slid across a satin cheek, found warm, sweet lips….

"Don't," the girl struggled. "Let me down. They—they'll come to and…."

She was on her feet. "You're right," Red Finger groaned. "You're right, Flower." He turned. "We have no right to—" He was dialling a number on the telephone. "They'll stay out for half-an-hour, but we've got to get away. Even the D.J. must not know who we are." A voice answered him on the 'phone, and he was spitting terse sentences into the transmitter. "Room two-fifty, Hotel Winston. Three men. Dictograph record outside the window. Hurry. Orders of G-1, Washington."

"Yes, sir," the voice answered him, suddenly respectful. "At once." Red Finger thumped the receiver into its cradle.

"Flower," he said, twisting, "We…." And cut off.

There was no one else in the room. No one but the three on the floor. Of the girl there was only the faint, elusive scent of the perfume of a rose, drifting in the air.

Curiously, Ho Chien's still, saffron face seemed to smile, with a queer triumph. He seemed to be saying, "The hand that wields

232

a swo'd may not pick a blossom. The mountain path is nallow, the'e is not loom fo' two upon it."

There were only the three unconscious men in the room when the Department of Justice agents arrived. No one in the Hotel Winston could tell them who it was that had telephoned from there.

POPULAR HERO PULPS AVAILABLE NOW:

THE SPIDER
❏ #1: The Spider Strikes	$13.95
❏ #2: The Wheel of Death	$13.95
❏ #3: Wings of the Black Death	$13.95
❏ #4: City of Flaming Shadows	$13.95
❏ #5: Empire of Doom!	$13.95
❏ #6: Citadel of Hell	$13.95
❏ #7: The Serpent of Destruction	$13.95
❏ #8: The Mad Horde	$13.95
❏ #9: Satan's Death Blast	$13.95
❏ #10: The Corpse Cargo	$13.95
❏ #11: Prince of the Red Looters	$13.95
❏ #12: Reign of the Silver Terror	$13.95
❏ #13: Builders of the Dark Empire	$13.95
❏ #14: Death's Crimson Juggernaut	$13.95
❏ #15: The Red Death Rain	$13.95
❏ #16: The City Destroyer	$13.95
❏ #17: The Pain Emperor	$13.95
❏ #18: The Flame Master	$13.95
❏ #19: Slaves of the Crime Master	$13.95
❏ #20: Reign of the Death Fiddler	$13.95
❏ #21: Hordes of the Red Butcher	$13.95
❏ #22: Dragon Lord of the Underworld	$13.95
❏ #23: Master of the Death-Madness	$13.95
❏ #24: King of the Red Killers	$13.95
❏ #25: Overlord of the Damned	$13.95
❏ #26: Death Reign of the Vampire King	$13.95
❏ #27: Emperor of the Yellow Death	$13.95
❏ #28: The Mayor of Hell	$13.95
❏ #29: Slaves of the Murder Syndicate	$13.95
❏ #30: Green Globes of Death	$13.95
❏ #31: The Cholera King	$13.95
❏ #32: Slaves of the Dragon	$13.95
❏ #33: Legions of Madness	$12.95
❏ #34: Laboratory of the Damned	$12.95
❏ #35: Satan's Sightless Legion	$12.95
❏ #36: The Coming of the Terror	$12.95
❏ #37: The Devil's Death-Dwarfs	$12.95
❏ #38: City of Dreadful Night	$12.95
❏ #39: Reign of the Snake Men	$12.95
❏ #40: Dictator of the Damned	$12.95
❏ #41: The Mill-Town Massacres	$12.95
❏ #42: Satan's Workshop	$12.95
❏ #43: Scourge of the Yellow Fangs	$12.95
❏ #44: The Devil's Pawnbroker	$12.95
❏ #45: Voyage of the Coffin Ship	$12.95
❏ #46: The Man Who Ruled in Hell	$13.95
❏ #47: Slaves of the Black Monarch	$13.95

❏ #48: Machineguns Over the White House	$13.95
❏ #49: The City That Dared Not Eat	$13.95
❏ #50: Master of the Flaming Horde	$13.95
❏ #51: Satan's Switchboard	$13.95
❏ #52: Legions of the Accursed Light	$13.95
❏ #53: The City of Lost Men	$13.95
❏ #54: The Grey Horde Creeps	$13.95
❏ #55: City of Whispering Death	$13.95
❏ #56: When Thousands Slept in Hell	$13.95
❏ #57: Satan's Shakles	$14.95
❏ #58: The Emperor From Hell	$14.95
❏ #59: The Devil's Candlesticks	$14.95
❏ #60: The City That Paid to Die	$14.95
❏ #61: The Spider at Bay	$14.95
❏ #62: Scourge of the Black Legions	$14.95
❏ #63: The Withering Death	$14.95
❏ #64: Claws of the Golden Dragon	$14.95
❏ #65: The Song of Death	$14.95
❏ #66: The Silver Death Reign	$14.95
❏ #67: Blight of the Blazing Eye	$14.95
❏ #68: King of the Fleshless Legion	$14.95
❏ *NEW:* #69: Rule of the Monster Men	$16.95

THE WESTERN RAIDER
❏ #1: Guns of the Damned	$13.95
❏ #2: The Hawk Rides Back from Death	$13.95
❏ #3: Gun-Call for the Lost Legion	$13.95
❏ #4: The Law of Silver Trent	$13.95
❏ #5: The Gun-Prayer of Silver Trent	$13.95
❏ #6: Silver Trent Rides Alone	$13.95

G-8 AND HIS BATTLE ACES
❏ #1: The Bat Staffel	$13.95

CAPTAIN SATAN
❏ #1: The Mask of the Damned	$13.95
❏ #2: Parole for the Dead	$13.95
❏ #3: The Dead Man Express	$13.95
❏ #4: A Ghost Rides the Dawn	$13.95
❏ #5: The Ambassador From Hell	$13.95

DR. YEN SIN
❏ #1: Mystery of the Dragon's Shadow	$12.95
❏ #2: Mystery of the Golden Skull	$12.95
❏ #3: Mystery of the Singing Mummies	$12.95

RED FINGER
❏ *NEW:* #1: Second-Hand Death	$24.95

POPULAR HERO PULPS AVAILABLE NOW:

ACE G-MAN
- ❏ #1: The Suicide Squad Reports for Death $14.95
- ❏ #2: Coffins for the Suicide Squad $14.95
- ❏ #3: Shells for the Suicide Squad $14.95
- ❏ #4: The Suicide Squad in Corpse-Town $14.95
- ❏ #5: Wanted–In Three Pine Coffins $14.95
- ❏ #6: The Suicide Squad's Dawn Patrol $14.95

OPERATOR 5
- ❏ #1: The Masked Invasion $13.95
- ❏ #2: The Invisible Empire $13.95
- ❏ #3: The Yellow Scourge $13.95
- ❏ #4: The Melting Death $13.95
- ❏ #5: Cavern of the Damned $13.95
- ❏ #6: Master of Broken Men $13.95
- ❏ #7: Invasion of the Dark Legions $13.95
- ❏ #8: The Green Death Mists $13.95
- ❏ #9: Legions of Starvation $13.95
- ❏ #10: The Red Invader $13.95
- ❏ #11: The League of War-Monsters $13.95
- ❏ #12: The Army of the Dead $13.95
- ❏ #13: March of the Flame Marauders $13.95
- ❏ #14: Blood Reign of the Dictator $13.95
- ❏ #15: Invasion of the Yellow Warlords $13.95
- ❏ #16: Legions of the Death Master $13.95
- ❏ #17: Hosts of the Flaming Death $13.95
- ❏ #18: Invasion of the Crimson Death Cult $13.95
- ❏ #19: Attack of the Blizzard Men $13.95
- ❏ #20: Scourge of the Invisible Death $13.95
- ❏ #21: Raiders of the Red Death $13.95
- ❏ #22: War-Dogs of the Green Destroyer $13.95
- ❏ #23: Rockets From Hell $13.95
- ❏ #24: War-Masters from the Orient $13.95
- ❏ #25: Crime's Reign of Terror $13.95
- ❏ #26: Death's Ragged Army $13.95
- ❏ #27: Patriots' Death Battalion $13.95
- ❏ #28: The Bloody Forty-five Days $13.95
- ❏ #29: America's Plague Battalions $13.95
- ❏ #30: Liberty's Suicide Legions $13.95
- ❏ #31: Siege of the Thousand Patriots $13.95
- ❏ #32: Patriots' Death March $14.95
- ❏ #33: Revolt of the Lost Legions $14.95
- ❏ #34: Drums of Destruction $14.95
- ❏ #35: The Army Without a Country $14.95
- ❏ #36: The Bloody Frontiers $14.95
- ❏ #37: The Coming of the Mongol Hordes $14.95
- ❏ *NEW:* #38: The Siege That Brought the Black Death $16.95

CAPTAIN COMBAT
- ❏ #1: The Sky Beast of Berlin $13.95
- ❏ #2: Red Wings For the Blood Battalion $13.95
- ❏ #3: Low Ceiling For Nazi Hell Hawks $13.95

DUSTY AYRES AND HIS BATTLE BIRDS
- ❏ #1: Black Lightning! $13.95
- ❏ #2: Crimson Doom $13.95
- ❏ #3: The Purple Tornado $13.95
- ❏ #4: The Screaming Eye $13.95
- ❏ #5: The Green Thunderbolt $13.95
- ❏ #6: The Red Destroyer $13.95
- ❏ #7: The White Death $13.95
- ❏ #8: The Black Avenger $13.95
- ❏ #9: The Silver Typhoon $13.95
- ❏ #10: The Troposphere F-S $13.95
- ❏ #11: The Blue Cyclone $13.95
- ❏ #12: The Tesla Raiders $13.95

MAVERICKS
- ❏ #1: Five Against the Law $12.95
- ❏ #2: Mesquite Manhunters $12.95
- ❏ #3: Bait for the Lobo Pack $12.95
- ❏ #4: Doc Grimson's Outlaw Posse $12.95
- ❏ #5: Charlie Parr's Gunsmoke Cure $12.95

THE MYSTERIOUS WU FANG
- ❏ #1: The Case of the Six Coffins $12.95
- ❏ #2: The Case of the Scarlet Feather $12.95
- ❏ #3: The Case of the Yellow Mask $12.95
- ❏ #4: The Case of the Suicide Tomb $12.95
- ❏ #5: The Case of the Green Death $12.95
- ❏ #6: The Case of the Black Lotus $12.95
- ❏ #7: The Case of the Hidden Scourge $12.95

THE SECRET 6
- ❏ #1: The Red Shadow $13.95
- ❏ #2: House of Walking Corpses $13.95
- ❏ #3: The Monster Murders $13.95
- ❏ #4: The Golden Alligator $13.95

CAPTAIN ZERO
- ❏ #1: City of Deadly Sleep $13.95
- ❏ #2: The Mark of Zero! $13.95
- ❏ #3: The Golden Murder Syndicate $13.95

www.ingramcontent.com/pod-product-compliance
Lightning Source LLC
Chambersburg PA
CBHW030538030726
47495CB00004B/1036